THE CASE OF THE
MURDERED MODEL

THE "MAC" SERIES

Draw the Curtain Close (1947)
Every Bet's a Sure Thing (1953)
The Case of the Murdered Model (1954, aka *Prey for Me*)
The Mean Streets (1954)
The Brave, Bad Girls (1956)
You've Got Him Cold (1958)
The Case of the Chased and the Chaste (1959)
How Hard to Kill (1962)
A Sad Song Singing (1963)
Don't Cry for Long (1964)
Portrait of a Dead Heiress (1965)
Deadline (1966)
Death and Taxes (1967)
The King Killers (1968, aka *Death Turns Right*)
The Love-Death Thing (1969)
The Taurus Trip (1970)

THE PETE SCHOEFIELD SERIES:

And When She Stops (1957 aka *I.O.U. Murder*)
Go To Sleep, Jeannie (1959)
Too Hot For Hawaii (1960)
The Golden Hooligan (1961, aka *Mexican Slayride*)
Go, Honeylou (1962)
The Girl with the Sweet Plump Knees (1963)
The Girl in the Punchbowl (1964)
Only on Tuesdays (1964)
Nude in Nevada (1965)

THE CASE OF THE
MURDERED MODEL

THOMAS B. DEWEY

CHAPTER 1

I dreamed the telephone was ringing. It rang and rang and I turned over to make it stop. But it went on and pretty soon I was awake. My watch read two-eighteen—in the A. M. I picked up the phone.

"Yuh," I said.

Came a heavy voice with a trace of Irish in it.

"Mac, I'm sittin' up with a dead lady and I'm lonesome. Come on over."

He hung up. I hung up, too, and pulled the covers around my neck.

Sure, I thought. Come on over. Come on over to in Christ's name where?

It rang again and I grabbed it. The same Irish voice said, "Better come on over, son. The address is Apartment eight-o-five. Right around the corner."

"Listen, Donovan," I said, "it's two-thirty in the morning—"

"I said I'm sittin' up with a dead lady."

"I'm sorry when somebody dies—"

"She's a client of yours. I thought you'd like to know."

The phone went dead.

I lay there a minute, holding it in my hand, and then slowly I put it back in the cradle, rolled out of bed and began to dress. My mouth felt full of cotton and I took time to brush my teeth. I'd gone to bed only a couple of hours before and my eyes were raw and gritty. I put some drops in them, found my hat, straightened my tie and went outside.

Fog floated around the lamp posts and a cold wind blew off the Lake—three blocks away and behind me as I walked toward Michigan Avenue. There were a few late stragglers on the walks and now and then a car passed. But most of the buildings were dark and, except for the distant rumble of a truck and an occasional blast from a foghorn on the river, the city was quiet.

I walked to Michigan, turned north and went on to Walton Place, a quiet, residential street, on the swanky side. Now, in the first block off the Boulevard, it was deserted. But farther on, in the second block, I saw police cars in front of a high apartment building. Across the street were more cars and a small knot of men milling around with a couple of uniformed cops holding them in check. There was a young cop in uniform at the apartment house door.

"Live here, sir?" he asked.

"No, sir," I said. "Donovan sent for me."

He looked doubtful. He stuck his head inside the door and another cop looked out. The youngster spoke to him and the inside man nodded, then held the door open as I stepped into the foyer. There was the small explosion of a flash bulb across the street and I pointed over there.

"Hello, Mac," the cop said. "Hell of a night."

I nodded, embarrassed because I couldn't remember his name.

"Those gentlemen across the street," I said. "They're from the press?"

"Those gentlemen," he said bitterly.

Still embarrassed, I slapped his shoulder and went on toward an automatic elevator at the end of the foyer. The cop called after me.

"Eighth floor, Mac. Turn to the right."

It was a clean, well-kept place with thick carpeting and a modern decor. The elevator was down and except for the muffled clang of the door, it made no sound rising. I was alone in it and I leaned against the wall, wishing I were back in bed, hating the thought of death and the people who came to it in this disorderly, inconvenient way.

As I stepped out on the eighth floor, I faced a short corridor that ran toward the front of the building. A longer hall intersected it and ran to my right and my left. There were doors on both sides. They were all closed except for a door far down to my right. This was open and light fell out of it onto the thick carpet of the corridor. Another cop sat on a straight chair just outside the open door.

This one didn't know me either and he had to go inside and check while I stood in the hall and waited.

"You can go on in," he said when he came back.

I went past him into the apartment.

It was spacious and well-appointed and the rent was maybe three hundred a month. There was a small vestibule with a wall on my left and a chest-high rail on my right with a long planter on top. Looking through the foliage across the rail I could see into a large living room, with comfortable, modern furniture and the outer edges of a nine-by-twelve white shag rug. As always at such times, the room seemed full of people.

Two plain-looking plainclothesmen from Lieutenant Donovan's squad were wandering around. A photographer had a camera set up on a tripod just off the white shag rug and his bored assistant dangled a sack of flash-bulbs. Two quiet, efficient men in shirtsleeves from the police lab were going over the room with various items of equipment. Once in a while somebody spoke in a low, muffled tone and once in a while somebody

6

would answer. But never loudly. The only off-key note in the place was the light. Part of it came from the photographer's flood lamp and part from an overhead fixture with a flaring shade that threw light down in a wide circle onto the floor below. It hurt my eyes.

I didn't see Donovan till I got past the planter rail, leaving a dinette behind me as I turned into the living room. Donovan sat on one end of a long davenport against the wall. Behind him were three high windows over which Venetian blinds had been dropped and closed. His hat was pushed back on his head and his hands lay loosely on his thighs. He stared into space, looking morose, as if everybody had it in for him. His squat, wide-shouldered frame sat stiff and straight and his right foot was twisted and lay on edge on the floor. Now and then he tapped his left foot on the floor, slowly in a measured rhythm. His mouth worked a little.

At the other end of the davenport sat a young man who didn't fit in with the rest of the people. He was young—maybe twenty—dressed in a dark, expensive suit, with a white carnation in the lapel. He had a sensitive, pale face with large brown eyes and a long, slightly curved nose. He sat rigid on the davenport with his hands in his lap and looked steadily away from Donovan and from whatever was going on in the middle of the room.

I walked over to Donovan.

"Hello, copper," I said.

He glanced up, then looked away.

"Hello, shamus," he said.

I waited a minute.

"What am I doing here?" I asked.

Donovan's mouth twitched. He made a left-handed gesture toward the middle of the room.

The two plainclothesmen had stopped pacing and were watching me. The photographer stared at me as he worked over his camera. The helper and the two lab men didn't pay any attention. I looked at the camera to see what it was aimed at.

It was aimed at the white shag rug and the photographer might have been the artistic type, preparing to shoot a posing model against a traditional background. Only I knew he was a police photographer and that all the other guys in the room, except for the kid on the davenport, were cops, and it wasn't hard to tell that the model was not posing of her own free will, because she did not have any free will left.

She lay on her back, with her left knee drawn up, resting against her right thigh. She was completely nude. Her arms were flung out on both sides, and her face looked at the ceiling. Already there was a bluish tinge to her lips. There was no trace of makeup on her face, but a faint sheen here and there, as from cold cream. High on her left temple, where the hair had been drawn back to disclose it, was a livid, swollen bruise. The skin was not broken, and unless she had fallen against something, the bruise would have been made by a very blunt instrument. There did not seem to be anything against which she could have fallen.

She had been very beautiful. She had firm, tanned skin. Her hair was thick, glossy and dark, almost black but a little brown too under the light. Except for the bruise on her head and a small mole in the hollow of her throat, there were no blemishes of any kind. Her features were well rounded in the right places and clean cut. She had been maybe five feet, four inches tall. Once she must have looked like the kind of woman who could live in an apartment like this one and feel at home. But now she was dead. Her hair was tangled under her head. Her eyes were half-closed and the pupils glinted strangely under her lids and were without shape.

I had never seen her before in my life.

CHAPTER 2

As I turned back to Donovan I saw that the handsome kid on the other end of the davenport was watching me. He looked away when I caught his eye.

"What's her name?" I asked Donovan.

He shrugged.

"You ought to know," he said.

"No," I said firmly. "I don't know. What was it you told me on the phone?"

He made another gesture toward the wall to his left.

I looked over there. There was a small, bleached mahogany desk, flat topped, with drawers on each side and a kneehole between them. On top of the desk was an open classified telephone directory. I could tell in advance I didn't want to look at it.

"What's in it?" I said.

"Have a look," Donovan said.

His mouth worked some more. He was itching for me to look at the phone book, but he was too stubborn to say so. He'd wait if it took till dawn. I played with the thought of letting him wait, but then I looked at the two plainclothesmen with him and decided not to embarrass him.

I started on the trip to the desk, skirting the white rug, not looking at it as I passed. A faint fragrance of perfume lingered near it. I was thinking, Don't the old ever die? the beat-up, the twisted, the ugly?

And I thought, No, only the young and beautiful and strong.

And then I quit thinking about it because it was the kind of thinking that never gets you anywhere in my business.

Everybody in the room had stopped working to watch me. Even the lab men, half-stopped, had their eyes on me as I reached the desk. The photographer had twisted his gadget around and, looking back over my shoulder, I saw that it was now aimed at me. I looked at Donovan. As I opened my mouth to speak, a flashbulb exploded in my face. I stood there, waiting till the glare had died away.

"What does he do with those pictures?" I said, "sell them to the papers? He'll get a wide price for a shot of that girl on the rug."

9

The photographer was very busy with his camera. Donovan got up and walked over to him.

"Give me the holder," Donovan said.

The photographer stared at him.

"I thought you'd want—" he said.

"Give me the holder," Donovan repeated. "You know what you're shootin'. Get your goddam machine turned around the other way."

The photographer shrugged, pulled the film holder out of the back of the camera and handed it to Donovan. Donovan opened it, tore the film out and crumpled it in his hand. He gave the holder back to the photographer and threw the ruined film into a corner of the room. Then he returned to his seat on the davenport.

I glanced at the open directory, but couldn't bring myself to read in it. I glanced at the girl on the floor, the dead, beautiful girl with the rich dark hair and the lovely face with the now strange-looking eyes. I looked around the room.

The two city detectives could hardly hold onto themselves. Their hands clenched and relaxed jerkily at their sides. The two lab men had gone back to work, but they looked up furtively every few seconds, waiting for me to do something. The photographer stared at me while he put a new film holder in his camera. Donovan sat with his foot on edge and his beefy hands clasped on his lap, leaning forward a little but not looking at me. The handsome kid in the dark suit was gazing at me with his lips parted. The silence was complete and frightening.

I cleared my throat.

"If you gentlemen will excuse me—" I said.

Donovan rubbed a hand over his big, broken face.

"Shamus—" he said quietly, "look at the goddam phone book."

"Sure," I said. "I'll look. But I would like to say right now, I never saw that girl before in my life."

Donovan said nothing.

I bent over the desk. The directory was open to the heading, DETEC-TIVE AGENCIES. The big, familiar names were there: Burns, Hargrave, Pinkerton, etc. Also, naturally, my own. But unlike the others, my own name was marked. There was a black ring around it, made hastily with a soft pencil. My phone number was underscored. No other name under that heading was marked.

I straightened slowly.

"Well, what do you know?" I said, unable to think of any more suitable remark.

The fact that I had looked at the listing seemed to break a spell. I turned at the sound of heavy footsteps and found myself face to face with one of Donovan's bully boys. This was an overgrown, heavy-jowled guy who was new on Donovan's squad. His name, as I remembered it, was Robinson. He could hardly wait to get at me.

"O. K., Sir Galahad," he said, "who was she?"

He stood so close to me that either I would have to back up or he would have to pull in his stomach. I knew that if I backed up he would keep coming, so I stood still and we rubbed stomachs for a while. It was no great thrill for me.

"I told you," I said, "I never saw her before."

"When you talked to her on the phone," he said, "who was she?"

The other cop had approached and stood now just behind Robinson, looking over his shoulder at me.

"She never called me," I said.

"When you called her."

"Oh hell," I said. "You want to look in my phone book?"

I was trying to be patient, because it was normal that, showing off in front of Donovan, they would try to crowd me. I could let them crowd me a long time, as long as they would keep their hands off me. But if one of them should touch me, I knew I would let him have it and I would probably get hurt and anyway, Donovan would be on a spot. So I thought Donovan would keep them from crowding me too far. Still, it was nothing I could count on.

Robinson was glaring at me across his stomach.

"Let's start over," I said. "You asked me who she was. I said I didn't know. I still don't."

"She marked your name in the book," the other cop said over Robinson's shoulder.

Somebody came into the apartment, but I couldn't see past Robinson. The voice of the cop from downstairs spoke, "The reporters want in," he said.

Donovan snarled at him.

"Sure," Donovan said. "They got a nude woman dead in a fancy apartment. Sure they want in."

There was the sound of retreating footsteps and Donovan spoke plaintively into the air.

"I wonder where that doctor is?"

Robinson was still glaring at me.

"Come on, Mac," he said, "give us a big, fat break. Tell us who she was."

His partner put in a penny's worth.

"The bright boy has maybe forgot," he said.

I was getting sore. Not sore enough to swing on them, but plenty sore.

"Lay off," I said.

"Oh yeah?" Robinson said brilliantly.

"Then goodnight," I said.

I moved away, pushing past Robinson. He grabbed my arm and jerked on it. I started a swing from my knees. Then a heavy hand caught my arm and Donovan was between us.

"Break it up," Donovan said. He jerked his head at the two cops. "Go talk to that apartment manager again," he said. "Maybe she's pulled herself together."

"O. K.," Robinson said. "But listen, Lieutenant—some day, will you let me work this guy over?"

Donovan had a tired look in his eyes.

"Get goin'," he said.

The two of them walked away and went out of the apartment. One of the lab men came over and spoke to Donovan.

"Think we've got enough?" he said.

"How in hell would I know?" Donovan said. "Stick around a while."

"Want any more pictures?" the photographer asked.

"Wrap it up and beat it."

The photographer and his helper began to take down the camera. Donovan turned and stared vacantly at the girl on the white shag rug. I glanced at the boy on the davenport. He was watching me and when I looked at him, he looked away. Then suddenly he erupted from the davenport and took a step toward Donovan. His voice was thin, pitched on the edge of hysteria.

"Can't you at least put a sheet over her or something?" he yelled. "For God's sake!"

Donovan turned ponderously to look at him and spoke almost kindly.

"Take it easy, son."

"Can I go now?" the kid asked.

"What's your name?" Donovan said.

"I told you."

"Tell me again."

"Norman Krupp."

"Where do you live?"

"On Oglesby Avenue, on the South Side."

"With your folks?"

"Yes, with my folks. Who else?"

"Where do you work?"

"I'm a graduate student at the University of Chicago."

"Did your folks know you was runnin' around with this girl?"

Donovan gestured toward the girl on the rug. Norman Krupp's face was frantic now, his sensitive lips twisted.

"Yes, they knew! What's wrong with it?"

"Take it easy, son," Donovan said again. "You are the one that called the cops?"

"I told you all this before!"

"I know. You had a key to this apartment?"

"Yes."

"And how long was it after you got here tonight before you called the cops?"

"I don't remember—ten, fifteen minutes."

"Why was it so long?"

For the first time, the kid's eyes fell away from Donovan's.

"I—because I couldn't believe it. I couldn't believe she was dead. I thought she'd fainted or something."

"And you tried to bring her around?"

The kid's voice broke.

"Yes. I tried."

Donovan studied him for a few seconds and the kid began to stare at me. Then he seemed to tear his eyes away to gaze at the open directory on the little desk.

"I guess you better go home, son," Donovan said. "We'll want to talk to you tomorrow."

The boy opened his mouth to say something, but nothing came out. He turned quickly and headed across the room toward the door.

"Jackson!" Donovan called.

The young cop who was stationed at the door came into the room.

"The kid named Krupp," Donovan said, "is just leaving. Take him out the back way to miss the reporters. Then go down to the manager's apartment and put Robinson on his tail."

The cop went out fast, without seeming to hurry. Donovan and I were alone in the room except for the two lab men, who were prowling around trying to look busy. A young man in glasses and a tweed suit walked into the apartment. He carried a black bag. He came part way into the room and stopped, looking at Donovan.

"Davis, from the Coroner's office," he said.

"Pleased to meet you," Donovan said. "The problem is on the rug."

The young doctor went to the rug, took off his coat and folded it carefully before laying it on the floor beside him. He knelt down, opened his bag and started a routine examination of the dead girl. Donovan beckoned to one of the lab men, who came over.

"You better get back and run through whatever you got," Donovan said. "If there's a lot of different prints, maybe you could send them off to Washington tonight. The Krupp kid's draft board might have a set of his."

The lab man nodded and rejoined his companions. They picked up their kits and pretty soon they were gone. The young medical examiner was still kneeling beside the body. Donovan turned to look down at him.

"Why did she die?" Donovan asked.

The doctor glanced up. Because of his glasses, it was hard to know what he was looking at.

"I guess it must have been because her heart stopped beating," he said.

Donovan looked at me.

"Only to a doctor is murder a joke," he said.

"Relax, Lieutenant," the doctor said. "We'll get the answers for you."

"Uh-huh," Donovan said.

The young man was a little scared because of the way he had spoken to Donovan and he went back to work self-consciously.

"Let's go get a cup of coffee," Donovan said to me.

"Sure," I said.

I followed him out the door, down the hall, into the elevator and downstairs. Just outside the front door, the two cops I'd seen first stood at bay with a ring of reporters pressing them.

"They made it across the street," I said.

Donovan cursed under his breath.

We went to the door and one of the cops opened it for us. I followed Donovan to the sidewalk where he stopped. The reporters moved in around us.

"A lady has got killed," Donovan said. "I don't know how and I don't know who did it."

Flashbulbs started going off beyond the reporters' shoulders. Donovan blinked against them.

"What was her name?" a reporter asked.

"No identification," Donovan said.

One of them said loudly, "What's Mac doing here? You call him in, Lieutenant?"

Donovan's face worked violently.

"I called him," he said, "but not *in*—not the way you mean."

Another reporter said, "You mean he's here for questioning?"

"I said what I mean," Donovan said. "Come around in the morning and maybe I'll have some more."

He pushed through them. One of the cops had come down from the door to help us. The reporters followed us to one of the squad cars and crowded around as we climbed into the back seat. One of them yelled something as the car pulled away from the curb, but I couldn't make it out.

"You said she got killed," I said to Donovan. "Do you know this?"

He shrugged heavily.

"Does a girl like that just lay down on the rug and die?" he said.

I kept quiet. The driver went fast through the dark, damp streets. He turned west on Chicago Avenue and pulled in suddenly when Donovan spoke to him. I opened the door and climbed out. There was a taxi three or four cars behind us. It backed slowly into the curb and the lights went out. Where it had stopped, the streets were dark and deserted. It was no place to discharge a fare and it was no cab stand either. I didn't mention it to Donovan.

CHAPTER 3

We sat down in a rear booth of an all-night cafe. There was a newsboy at the counter up front, but no other customers. Donovan ordered coffee and the waitress yawned at us as she set it down. After a while, Donovan said, "All right, we're alone now. You can talk."

"No I can't," I said, "because I don't have anything to talk about."

Donovan ran a hand down over his face.

"How can you figure I knew her?" I said.

"She knew about you."

"I've been in the papers."

Donovan finished his coffee and ordered a refill. He got halfway through the second cup before he spoke again and by that time he was talking to himself as much as to me.

"I wish I knew who she was," he said. "The manager of the building wasn't no help. She's a snotty dame—also nervous. Couldn't bring herself to view the remains. Said the apartment was leased to a girl named Marta Sandor."

"Then you've got a start," I said. "What did the Krupp boy tell you?"

"He used the same name—Marta Sandor. Said she used another one too. Diana—Peterson."

"What name did she use on the mailbox?"

"No name. Just the apartment number. Sometimes they do that—like an unlisted telephone number."

"How long has young Krupp known her?"

"He says about three months."

"Passionate affair?"

Donovan shrugged.

"Said they went out together—maybe once a week."

"She had other boyfriends?"

"What do you think?"

"I never met her. I only saw her dead."

Donovan drank some more coffee.

"That manager didn't even know where she worked."

"Didn't she have any papers? Social Security, driver's license—?"

"No papers. No bank book. There was eight or nine hundred bucks in cash in a black velvet purse. That's all—the money, a white lace handkerchief and a pair of black net gloves."

"Any other purses in the place?"

"Sure other purses. Empty."

I finished my coffee and stood up.

"Well, good luck, copper," I said. "If you want me, you know where to find me."

"Wait a minute," he said, and I sat down again.

He was having the trouble with his face that he always had when he was about to ask a favor of me. I would have tried to help him, but I didn't have any idea what to expect. Finally he got it out.

"There was another name marked in that phone book."

"You don't say."

Donovan pulled out a small notebook, leafed through it, found what he wanted and looked up at me.

"Ben Champlain," he said. "A commercial photographer."

"That fits," I said.

"Fits what?"

"The condition in which you found her."

Donovan put the notebook away.

"I was thinking," he said, not looking at me now, "if you was to go see this guy—this Ben Champlain—"

"Me?"

"Yeah. Both your names marked in the book that way. See, if I go right off, being a cop and all—" I stared at him.

"He would speak more freely to me," I said. "Is that it?"

"Yeah. After all—both the names—maybe there's some connection. I could probably get an appropriation to pay for your time. Fifty bucks—"

"You want me to talk to this photographer and then peddle the information to you—for fifty bucks?"

"That ain't what I said—"

"I heard what you said. Why do you think people go to private cops? No deal."

I got up again, turning away from the booth. Donovan walked with me to the door. He put a hand on my shoulder.

"Mac, son," he said quietly, "you sure you don't know this girl?"

"If you can think of something to swear by," I said, "I'll swear."

He looked me in the face for a while and I looked back at him. He was a great guy and I loved him, but I couldn't help him. Not this time.

"O. K., Shamus," he said. "You want a lift home?"

"Thanks, I'll walk," I said. "You've got your hands full."

I went to his car with him and slammed the door after he'd got in. He spoke to the driver and they moved into the street. Donovan waved briefly with a broad hand. I turned toward the lake and started the short walk back to my place.

The fog had grown heavier and the lights along the empty streets were faint glowing blobs. Traffic was at a standstill. I had that cold, closed-in feeling you get in a fog when all you can hear is your own footsteps on the walk and you can't see anything at all. I was sleepy and felt put upon, but I was glad not to be Donovan.

I came to a corner and the traffic light showed fuzzy green through the fog. I listened for traffic, heard none and went on across, feeling for the curb with one foot as I reached the other side.

The next block was a row of dingy store fronts, all of them dark, most of the places dark inside too, without night lights. I walked faster, think-ing of getting back to bed and trying to forget the girl on the white shag rug. I had seen death before, but I had never got used to it. This meant one more scene that I would be waking at night to remember. It would grow dimmer as time went by and after a while I would forget what the girl had really looked like. But it would never go away completely. They never do. They never will.

I felt a change in the atmosphere around me and remembered an alley that emptied into the street in this block. There was a short step down into it and I felt for it as I walked. I made it down, crossed the alley and stepped up onto the walk again. Then there were rapid footsteps close be-hind me and a taut voice spoke.

"Wait a minute!"

I didn't think it all through at the time, but it was a great night for mug-ging and I reacted without thinking. The footsteps had practically climbed up my back and I could feel the sudden warmth his body made when it moved close to me. I tightened all over as the startle-shock hit me in the stomach and chest, then pivoted toward the wall of the building nearby and struck out at the source of the voice.

I missed the face but connected with a shoulder. The blow spun him around and I could see his shape dimly now as I jammed him against the wall, trying to follow up with a right hand that would cool him quickly. But he wasn't struggling and before I could land another one, his voice came again, pleading.

"Please—wait!"

Then I placed him.

"Krupp," I said.

I held him with my hand against his chest. He leaned hard on the wall of the store and I could feel his heart pounding against my hand, but there was no fight left in him.

"What makes you jump out on a man that way?" I said.

It was some time before he could answer. Then his voice was thin and distant.

"I'm sorry," he said. "I had to talk to you."

"I've got an office."

"I know. I didn't know where it was."

"You were in that cab?"

"Yes."

"What did you have in mind?"

There was another long pause while he tried to pull himself together.

"I had to know why she marked your name," he said.

I took my hand off his chest and tried to look at him in the fog. I was close enough to him so that, if he had been drinking, I would have smelled it. But he hadn't been drinking.

"What is it to you?" I asked.

"It could be a lot to me."

He was awfully upset. His breath came harder than it should have from the brief exertion and the shock of my jumping him. I had felt him shaking when my hand was on him.

"Listen," he said, "I know about you."

"What do you know?"

"I know what I've heard. You're an honest man."

"Thanks," I said. "What will it cost me?"

"All I want to know is why she called you."

"She didn't call me. I said this before."

"But she marked your name in the book—" I tried to study his face through the murk, but couldn't see much of it.

"You'd better forget it and go on home," I said.

"I can't. There's a cop following me."

"How do you know?"

"I know. That Donovan wouldn't let me walk away without having me watched."

I couldn't deny it. But I couldn't do anything about it, either.

"Well," I said, "the cop won't try to get in bed with you."

"He'll hang around. It's embarrassing."

"You could expect to be embarrassed. It's embarrassing to be found in your dead girlfriend's apartment."

There was a longer pause this time, the longest of all. Then he said, "I was in love with her."

He said it straight and simply.

"All right," I said. "What's the pitch?"

19

"No pitch. I just thought she might have told you something—"

"How could she tell me anything? She never called me. I guess she didn't get around to it."

"Maybe if she had called you—this wouldn't have happened."

"Maybe. But it's no use thinking about that."

"I guess not."

"Where's your cab?"

"I sent it away."

It was cold on the street and he was making me jumpy. I stepped back away from him.

"You can pick up a cab at the corner," I said, "at Michigan. I'm walking that way."

I started off down the street. After a few paces I heard his steps behind me, hurrying to catch up. We walked rapidly side by side toward Michigan. I thought about him as we walked. He was no ordinary punk kid. He wore expensive clothes. He said he went to the University. The name Krupp wasn't uncommon and right then I couldn't connect him with anything familiar. But from what I had seen of him I would guess he had a good background, a solid home life with plenty of security in it. The girl on the white shag rug had probably been older—maybe ten years older—and he might have done her in after a quarrel. He was sensitive and high strung. If she'd run around a lot and if he'd thought he loved her, they could have plenty of quarrels on short notice. I guess it was Shakespeare who said men never died for love. But the police blotters are loaded with the names of men who had killed for love—or a reasonable facsimile of same.

It wasn't my case, I told myself. The only thing Donovan wanted from me was something I couldn't do.

Krupp didn't speak again till we got to the corner of Michigan and Chicago. There were two cabs parked near the drugstore, but we didn't see them till we had crossed the street. The kid stared at them for a minute and then he said, "I can't go home now."

"Sure you can go home. Why not?"

He shook his head.

"I'll go to the hotel down the street," he said.

He kept rubbing his forehead with his hands. They were pale in the dark and I saw they were shaking.

"I can't get it out of my mind," he said, "the way I walked in and found her—I can't—" His shoulders began to shake. I wondered whether he was putting on an act. If so, he ought to save it for Donovan. I took his arm and tried to lead him to one of the cabs. The driver saw us coming and got out to open the door. We were almost there when the kid jerked away from me and stepped back.

"No!" he said. "I can't—" I shrugged at the driver. He shrugged in return and after a moment got back in his cab and picked up the newspaper he had been reading. I turned to look at the boy.

"All right," I said, "it's up to you. But I'm going home to bed."

For a sadistic moment I had the hope that he would wander around the streets the rest of the night, causing Donovan's man, Robinson, to lose some of his belly. I looked back along the street, trying to spot the shadow, but I couldn't find him. I started off again toward home.

After a few steps, he caught up again and put his hand on my arm.

"Can't you even guess why she might have wanted to call you?"

"Look," I said, "I told you everything I know. Maybe she was afraid of something. Maybe you. Maybe she wanted help. But I never got the message. Maybe she died too soon."

This was unnecessarily brutal and like the tender heart I sometimes am, I felt sorry.

"If you have to go on talking about it," I said, "at least let me get in out of the cold."

"I'll buy you a drink," he said.

"You seem too young to drink. We'll go to my place."

"I'm twenty-one," he said as we started off again.

"Good for you."

I was sore now, mostly at myself, because I had him on my hands. I might have quite a lot on my hands. He'd said he was a graduate student at the University. If he was only twenty-one, that made him quite a bright boy. Bright boys are sometimes harder to get along with than dull ones.

Maybe, I thought, as I unlocked my door and switched on the light inside, I'm getting old.

CHAPTER 4

My office and apartment are run together, with the office in front and a bedroom, kitchen and bath in the rear. I gave the Krupp boy a chair near my desk and went to the kitchen for the brandy bottle. I felt chilled to the bone and still jumpy. I poured out two generous slugs of brandy and offered one to Krupp. He drank it down, gulped, then looked at me desperately and I showed him where the bathroom was. I waited in the office and when he came back he was paler than ever and shaking again.

"First drink?" I asked.

He shook his head.

"No. I'm upset."

"Well," I said, "would it be all right with you if we caught a little sleep? You can use the daybed in here."

"If you say so," he said.

I found a couple of blankets in my bedroom and put them out for him. He was still sitting straight up in the chair, staring into space. We were no doubt having the same mental image. But if he had been in love with her, his would be more horrifying than mine.

"What was her name?" I asked.

His bright eyes looked at mine.

"Marta," he said. "Marta Sandor."

"Then who was Diana Peterson?" I said.

He blinked at me.

"It was another name she used."

"You have any idea what she might have been scared about?"

He started to speak right up, then his eyes dropped, he looked away and shook his head.

"No," he said. "I don't know that she was frightened."

"I see. Well, I've got to go to bed. Make yourself comfortable."

"Goodnight," he said, still stiff on the chair, still staring into space.

Everything in the office was locked up tight, so I didn't worry about leaving him. I hoped he would go to sleep, but I didn't count on it for him. It took me a while to get to sleep myself, and then I kept waking up. The only good thing about the night was that each time I woke, I thought about Robinson, standing out in the fog, waiting for Krupp to leave.

* * * *

The last time I woke it was daylight and young Krupp was coming out of the bathroom. He was trying to be quiet, but he stumbled over a chair and I came awake in a hurry. My watch read seven-thirty.

"Better have some breakfast," I said and rolled out.

I made coffee and scrambled some eggs, while the Krupp kid sat in the kitchen, looking now and then at me, most of the time at nothing. When I served up the eggs, he picked at them a little but didn't eat much. He drank the coffee and I saw he was having to struggle over it.

"Does Lieutenant Donovan think I killed her?" he said.

"I don't know what Donovan thinks," I said, "but he is the greatest cop in the world."

"I didn't do it," he said. "I came in and found her—I couldn't have done it—no matter what."

"No matter *what* what?" I said.

"Even if she did—" He put his face in his hands.

"She went out with other guys?" I said.

He looked up again, angry.

"She was loyal and good," he said. "She'd had a hard life."

"How often did you see her?"

"Once a week. But that was all right. I have to study most of the time. She was going to marry me after I got my degree."

"But she wouldn't go steady with you."

He flared up.

"I wouldn't expect her to sit around all week doing nothing."

"Sure," I said. "I guess I'm old-fashioned."

He got up suddenly, bumping the table as he rose.

"I've got to go. I've got a ten o'clock class."

"You might be better off to cut it and get some more sleep," I said. "There's always a taxi across the street."

"I ran out of change," he said. "I'll have to take the I. C."

He's used to having money, I thought. He hadn't run out of money— only "change." It would be too bad to have to cash in a bond for a cab fare. If he lived on Oglesby Avenue on the South Side he couldn't get very close to it on the I. C.

I'm not sure even now why I made my next suggestion. I am not in the business of comforting or transporting bereaved youth. I owed this boy nothing. I stood to gain nothing except a little semi-fresh air and I stood to lose considerable time—though on this morning I hadn't yet picked up any work. It must have been curiosity—or a feeling of guilt that I hadn't offered Donovan any help. Anyway, I found myself saying, "I'll run you home in the car."

23

"I couldn't ask you," he said.

"All right. Wait till I get dressed."

He waited in the office while I dressed. The first mail had been dropped through the slot in my door and I looked through it hastily. There was nothing in it to occupy my time. I threw it on the desk and ushered Krupp outside. My car was parked at the curb in front and after a quick glance around, I spotted Robinson in front of the tavern across the street. I waved at him as we got into the car and pulled away. He didn't wave back.

The sun was fighting the fog, but traffic was snarled on Michigan and it took quite a while to get downtown and onto the Outer Drive. The boy didn't say anything till we were well on our way. Then, as usual, he shot me an abrupt question.

"What will they do with her?"

It took a few seconds for me to sort out what he meant.

"They'll find the nearest kin," I said, "and turn her over to them."

"But I mean right now—last night—when they took her away. What will they do with her?"

"I guess they'll take her to the morgue."

He shuddered violently.

"Will they perform an autopsy?" he asked.

"I don't know. That depends on what the coroner's man found out on the scene."

Pretty soon he said, "She didn't have any kin. They won't find any."

I didn't say anything. I wanted to stay out of it. After a while he spoke again.

"Could anybody claim her from the—morgue?"

I glanced at him.

"Like who for instance?" I said.

"Like me. I mean, can any citizen just—claim her?"

"Well, I guess so, if he wants to go to the trouble and expense."

"Would there be a lot of trouble?"

"Some red tape. Then, of course, there would be Donovan."

He shuddered again.

"Donovan," he said, making it sound hateful. "Would he use her body just as a pawn—just to find out who killed her?"

"Take it easy," I said.

But he was off again. His voice was furious now.

"To him she meant nothing," he said. "She was like dirt to him. Just an annoyance. Once he went over to look at her—I thought he was going to kick her in the face!"

24

He had started that shaking again. I would have to straighten him out before he broke down.

"Listen," I said, talking hard and fast, "there's a murder in the United States every hour of every day. A lot of them happen in Chicago. Most of those that happen in Chicago are Donovan's job."

"All right—"

"Shut up and listen. Put yourself in his shoes. What if every case he went out on was somebody he knew—a personal friend? What if he was in love with every woman who got killed—and he had to go and look at her and take pictures and try to figure out who did it? What if they were all people to him—people he'd known? How long could he stand it? How long could you stand it?"

He had his face in his hands again.

"I've known Donovan a long time," I said. "He's more of a father to me than the real one I had once. You think he's stone cold in here. You're wrong. Next to me he's probably the biggest softie in town. He gets no kick out of looking at corpses. But it's his job. He gets paid for it. Somebody has to do it."

"I'm sorry—"

"What if you had to do it? Would you have a nervous breakdown every time? Or would you figure out a way to protect yourself inside? Wouldn't you build a wall around that soft spot? You are goddam right you would. Or you would quit and go into some other business."

I laid off. I don't usually talk so much and I was a little embarrassed. I ran my finger around the inside of my collar and tried to cool down. I told myself I shouldn't flare up like that. But all I'd said about Donovan was true. And this kid was so young: so bright, so sensitive—and so young.

I reminded myself again: Don't get old, Mac. But he had rubbed me hard the wrong way and it took a long time to get back in balance. He didn't say anything more, fortunately, and he stopped shaking. I figured I'd braced him some and he could sure as hell use it. If he was bright enough, he could learn to talk about the thing he knew.

By the time we got out of Jackson Park and had crossed 67th Street, my fever had gone down and the boy was in better shape too. He showed me a shortcut to where he lived on Oglesby and I drove slowly along the tree-lined, comfortable street to his address.

It was a big house on a big lawn. A wide walk led back from the street between two stone pillars to the front door. I sat in the car, waiting for him to get out. He mumbled something, but I didn't catch it, because all of a sudden I had figured out who he was. Norman Krupp, only son of Aaron Krupp, who owned, if not the most famous, certainly the biggest and most lucrative department store in town. In addition, as I recalled from newspaper reports, he was chairman of the board of a store chain with units in every major city. Besides this, he was one of the best loved and most respected men in town. As a benefactor of the human race, he was in a class with Rosenwald and Guggenheim, and he had led more charity drives in and around Chicago than I would ever be able to count.

I wondered whether Donovan had known who young Krupp's father was and whether that had been the reason for avoiding the reporters. But I didn't have time to wonder for long, because a man was coming down the walk, through the pillars and after a slight pause, on to my car. He was tall and a little portly. He wore a gray homburg, a gray tweed suit and an ascot tie with a diamond stickpin. Thick white hair showed below the hat brim. He carried a folded newspaper under one arm. He walked with straight shoulders and great dignity.

He was Aaron Krupp.

CHAPTER 5

My passenger, Norman, had the door open and his feet on the walk by the time his father reached the car. I sat with my hands on the wheel, waiting. It was the old man who spoke first. His voice was deep and calm and he had a faint trace of accent.

"Good morning, son," he said.

"Hello, Papa," said Norman.

He waved his hand toward me vaguely, mentioned my name.

"He gave me a ride home," he said.

Aaron Krupp looked into the car and nodded.

"Thank you—for the boy," he said.

I nodded back.

"Don't mention it."

The two of them were standing now, looking at each other, and again it was the older who spoke.

"You should go up and let Mama see you're home," he said. "She worried a little."

"Yes, Papa," he said and moved off toward the house.

I reached for the door, to close it. The window was down and Aaron Krupp put his hand on the sill and looked in at me.

"You're going back toward the Loop?" he said.

"That's right."

He smiled a little. He had fine white teeth.

"Maybe you could give the boy's papa a lift?"

"Sure. Climb in."

He opened the door and slid in beside me, paying no attention to the frayed seat cover. He sat for a moment, gazing toward his house, where Norman was climbing the steps of the front porch. Then he looked at me.

"He has a class at ten o'clock," he said. "He studies chemistry. It's a good field."

"It's hard work."

He shrugged. He had big shoulders and the shrug was expressive, a part of his language—not just a sign of frustration, as with Donovan. I started the car and pulled away from the curb.

"He's a good boy," he said. "He works hard."

I found my way to a street that would take me to 67th Street and the entrance to Jackson Park. The elder Krupp sat looking straight ahead, holding the newspaper with both hands on his knees.

"You wouldn't believe it maybe," he said after a moment, "but the boy can cut and make a shirt—complete. Like that." He snapped his fingers. Then he laughed softly, as at a secret joke. "He don't have to make shirts, like I did, for fifteen years. In the old days in New York. But he knows how."

Pretty soon he spoke again, to himself, or to whatever he was looking at through the spotted windshield of my car.

"It's good to know things."

I kept driving. I was beginning to like the guy and I thought I ought to say something to let him know his boy was probably in a big fat jam, but I couldn't think of a way to say it and I kept feeling I wanted to stay out of it. After all, he wasn't doing me any favor by asking for a lift. Of course, he didn't act like he was doing me a favor. I had nothing to complain about.

We got into Jackson Park and Mr. Krupp opened his newspaper and spread it out across his knees. He looked at it for a while and then he said, "You took care of the boy—in the night?"

"He stayed at my place for a few hours," I said. "We had some breakfast. Then I brought him home. He ran out of cab fare."

"It was a favor," he said. "Thank you."

"Nothing," I said.

He looked at the paper some more. When he spoke again, he was serious, but without tragedy or dramatics.

"I see by the papers, a girl was killed. On Walton Place."

"Yes."

"Would this, by any chance, be a girl who called herself Marta Sandor?"

"That is the name I heard mentioned," I said.

He turned his head then and I knew he was looking at me, but I was too busy with traffic to look back. It gave him a slight advantage.

"That would be where you found my boy?"

"That was where I saw him for the first time."

"Did you know who he was?"

"No," I said. "I left the girl's apartment and the kid followed me. He stopped me on the street—on Chicago Avenue."

"And you took him home."

"He was upset. He didn't want to go home. There was a cop following him."

28

We were on the Outer Drive. There was a period of silence and then he said, "Do the police know what happened to the girl?"

"Only that she died," I said. "They think somebody killed her."

"Norman wouldn't kill," he said.

"I hope not."

"I know he was going with the girl. She wasn't a girl for him, but a boy has to find out for himself. He brought her once to the house."

"You didn't like her?"

"Like her—that's not the question. I might like her. You might like her. It's different. She was an older girl. Very glamorous to the boy."

"It hit him very hard," I said. "He wants to claim her body."

He removed his homburg, ran a hand around the band and replaced it on his head.

"So," he said, "if he wants to do that, let him do it."

"Means a lot of publicity," I said. "Sensational type."

He chuckled, but not with amusement; a dry, hard sound.

"I've had publicity. All kinds. It's important for the boy to do what he feels strongly."

"It's up to you," I said.

"But what about the girl's father?"

Traffic or no, I turned my head to look at him.

"I don't know," I said. "Your boy told me she had no kin."

"I think she had a father living."

I got my eyes back on the road.

"Do you know his name?" I asked.

He seemed to think about it.

"The name escapes me. I'll remember."

"When you remember," I said, "there's a cop who'd like to know about it. A lieutenant named Donovan."

"I'll try to remember," he said.

We were almost downtown now and I asked, "Where did you want to go?"

"If you will drop me on Michigan Avenue," he said, "I'll catch a taxi."

I maneuvered us into one of the lanes leading across to Michigan and we began to crawl. Krupp sat in silence for a while. He folded the newspaper and put it back under his arm. He straightened his ascot and adjusted the homburg.

"Mac," he said, "I hear a lot about you. All good."

"Thank you."

"It would be a favor to me—and to Mama—if you would take on the job."

"What job?" I was busy with the traffic.

"Excuse me. You should protect the boy's interests."

After the rambling way he'd been talking, this seemed very abrupt. I made the standard reply.

"If he's innocent," I said, "he has nothing to worry about."

"Even so," he said, "it would be a help if you would look into it."

"I don't know what I could do. Lieutenant Donovan—"

"A good policeman," Krupp said, "but part of a system." We were on the bridge, headed toward Michigan and traffic had backed up at the light. I relaxed behind the wheel and turned to look at him.

"Mr. Krupp," I said, "I'm no Sherlock Holmes. If your boy did not do the girl in, then Donovan will find it out eventually. In the meantime, he won't be persecuted, unless the papers smell out something they can play up. I can't protect him from the papers. For that you need a public-relations man. I'm only one step removed from a beat cop."

It was as if I hadn't said a word. While I talked, he had reached into a pocket and hauled out a checkbook in a green leather cover. He opened it on his knee and took out a pen.

"Two-hundred dollars," he said, "as a retainer. You will let me know when you need more. I heard what you said. I'm not buying anything— only your time. To help Donovan find out my boy didn't do it."

"What makes you so sure he didn't do it?"

He tore the check from the book and handed it to me. The sun had got through the fog now and glinted on the diamond stickpin in his ascot. He looked at me out of his big face.

"In my heart I know it," he said. "But I don't know the things to do. You know this kind of work. My job is minding the store."

He smiled. I looked at the check, put it in my pocket. I had plenty of doubts about what I could do for Norman Krupp. But as far as his old man was concerned, personally and as a guy I'd happened to run into, I was sold.

"If I can't do anything, I'll give it back," I said.

We had crossed the bridge now and were within half a block of the stoplight, where I would have to turn either left or right.

"I'll get out here," he said. "Thanks for the lift. You can call me at home or the office. I'm in the book."

"O. K., Mr. Krupp," I said.

He climbed out of the car and crossed quickly to the sidewalk. I watched him walk away, the newspaper under his arm, an erect figure, sure of himself in the best way. A man of dignity, with his boy in his heart.

CHAPTER 6

I parked my car in front of the office and crossed the street to pick up the papers, took them back to the office and checked in with my call service. There were three calls, two from insurance solicitors who should have known better. The third was from a *Tribune* reporter. I didn't want to call him, but I was afraid to ignore him. He wasn't in and I left my number so he would know I'd called. Then I spread the papers out on the desk and began to read about the death of Marta Sandor, for whom the reporters had no name.

You could read their frustration between the lines. They'd had their noses on a sensational scent and Donovan had led them through water. Some speculated wildly; others held it down to what they'd seen and heard. Somehow they'd heard she was found in a nude condition. This was the best break they'd had. The simple gist of all the stories was that an unidentified woman had been found dead in an apartment at 219 East Walton Place and that Lieutenant Donovan suspected foul play. My name was mentioned in two of the stories, but not in the others. In one of the late morning editions there was a bulletin on the case, stating that the Coroner's office would not announce the immediate cause of death until after an autopsy had been performed.

Norman Krupp's name was not mentioned. That meant he hadn't been seen, because he would certainly have been mentioned if any of the reporters had spotted and recognized him.

I put the papers away and tried to figure out what Aaron Krupp expected of me. I'd taken his money and I would have to earn it. But until something broke, until I found out more about the dead girl and why she'd been killed, there was nothing I do. Krupp couldn't expect me to solve the case single-handed.

Or could he?

If he did, then the best thing for me to do would be to take his check back to him and pull out of the assignment. But I had never done that before and this didn't look like the time to start.

One thing was sure. I would be running downhill as long as I could keep ahead of the cops. I figured I was neck and neck with Donovan now and maybe I could pull ahead.

I reached for the telephone and called Aaron Krupp's department store. It took a while to get him on the line and when he spoke I could tell he had someone with him. I gave him my name and asked, "Have you remembered the name of the girl's father?"

He cleared his throat.

"Shall I call you later?"

"No," he said. "His name is Peterson."

"Did you ever hear of a Diana Peterson?"

"I understand the girl used both names."

"Thanks," I said. "I won't bother you again."

"Any time," he said.

I broke the connection and sat for a minute with the phone in my hand. I had not got much of anywhere. Peterson was the name young Krupp had told me the girl had used, as if it had been a stage name. But "Marta Sandor" sounded more like a stage name than "Diana Peterson."

I dialed Donovan's private number. Normally he would be off duty at this hour of the morning, but on top of such a case, he might still be on the job.

Donovan's boy, Samuel, answered the phone and told me the Lieutenant was out. I told him I'd call later and hung up. I waited about five minutes and dialed again. This time Donovan answered.

"Short trip?" I said.

He growled at me.

"Maybe I have something you'd like to know," I said.

"Try it on me."

He sounded weary and disgruntled. He frequently sounded disgruntled, but there were different shades. This one showed he was missing his sleep.

"The girl had a father," I said.

"You don't say."

"His name is Peterson."

There was a pause and I visualized Donovan writing it down.

"All right, shamus," he said. "I got here the phone book. Which 'Peterson' is it?"

"Look, pop," I said, "the city doesn't pay me for this service."

"It ain't likely to. What else you got?"

"I was about to ask you."

"What do you care?"

"I'm patriotic. I like to help."

"Uh-huh. My man Robinson tells me you picked up young Krupp and took him in. Then you spirited him away somewhere and Robinson lost him."

"Oh?"

"I told Robinson, if he could think of a charge, he was welcome to bring you in."

"All right," I said, "but if that dumb flatfoot comes out here alone and raises his voice to me, he'll have to crawl back to City Hall on his hands and knees."

Donovan chuckled.

"That's my boy," he said. "Listen, Mac, is this straight, about the girl's old man?"

"I haven't checked it."

"Well, if we can find him, at least we'll have some place to send the body."

"Lieutenant," I said, "I have been thinking it over and I would like to do the police department a favor."

"Yeah?"

"I will be glad to call on this photographer—this Ben Champlain."

"The fifty bucks is out."

"I don't care about the fifty bucks."

"Of course, I already talked to Mr. Champlain."

"What did he say?"

"Nothin'. So I will pick him up and sweat him some. But not right away."

"Maybe he would talk to me."

"O. K.," Donovan said. "But if he does, don't make me sweat it out of you."

Since he was talking tough, I would have to hold up my end.

"On the best day you ever had," I said.

Donovan snorted.

"What killed the dead girl?" I asked.

"Suffocation," he said. "It took the coroner's office half a page of fancy words, single-spaced. But it boils down to suffocation."

"What about the bump on her head?"

"Didn't kill her. Just set her up for suffocation."

"With a pillow over her face?"

"I guess so."

"Did you find the blunt instrument?"

"Maybe."

"Find anything else in the apartment?"

"Just a little garbage—nice, ladylike garbage."

I took a deep breath and dived in. I had to try.

"How about letting me taking a look?" I asked.

After quite a while, Donovan said, "Who are you working for?"

"Forget it," I said.

"I guess there wouldn't be any harm in it. You won't find anything. But if you have to, go ahead and look."

"Be all right if I break in?"

"I'm pulling the guard off the place tonight at nine o'clock. I'll leave the door unlocked. I don't know whether the manager will lock it later or not."

"Why are you so good to me?"

"I don't know. But you might just be lucky enough to run across somethin'. In that case, naturally, you'll tell me about it."

"Naturally."

There was a loud knocking on my office door.

"See you later," I said. "I've got company."

"So long, shamus."

"So long, copper."

I hung up and went to the door. There were two men outside in the hall. One was beefy and sullen looking, with the scarred eyes and smashed nose of the fighter. He would have been in the heavyweight class, but since I didn't recognize him, he must have been short on the class.

The other guy was short and paunchy, with two chins, a soft looking belly and small, black eyes. There was a sharpness about him that suggested a promoter—a real fast promoter—and something familiar in his face, though I couldn't place it right away.

I didn't care for the looks of either, so I stood in the door and asked what they had in mind. The big one just stared over my head. The pudgy one stuck out a fat paw with an eighteen-carat diamond ring on the middle finger.

"I'm Barney Sorelle," he said. "I'd like to talk business."

"What kind of business?"

"Your kind."

He spoke up real snappy, as if he were used to getting things out of the way in a hurry. I looked away from him at the big guy with the face, who stared back at me gloomily.

"Are you partners?" I said.

The big one looked at Barney Sorelle and back at me. His mouth worked a little ahead of his words.

"I go everywhere he goes," he said slowly.

"Everywhere?"

I looked back at Sorelle, whose name at least meant something to me. I had never met him, so I hadn't connected the face with anything in my memory. Barney Sorelle was to Chicago what Mickey Cohen was to Los

Angeles, a kind of nuisance. He had some legitimate enterprises and then he had some others.

Still looking at Sorelle, I nodded toward the big one.

"Have him wait in the hall," I said.

Barney nodded to me and jerked his thumb at the bodyguard.

"But Barney—" the mug said.

"Do like I say!" Sorelle told him and the loyal lad backed away from the door and leaned against the banister of the stairway that led to the upper apartments. I stood aside to let Sorelle into the office, closing the door as I followed him to the desk. I indicated a chair and he sat down, whipped out two cigars and held one toward me. I shook my head. He clipped the end off one, stuck it in his mouth and lit up. I sat down at my desk.

"I'm in kind of a hurry," I said.

He leaned forward in the chair, chewing on the cigar and blowing out big puffs of smoke.

"Won't take long," he said. "I came to you because you got the best reputation in town. Discreet and all. Besides, you're in with the cops."

"Nobody's in with the cops," I said, "but go ahead."

"Last night," he said, "a girl died in an apartment on Walton Place. You were there. I read in the papers."

I stood up.

"I don't think we have any business to talk about," I said.

He ignored me. He puffed on the cigar and twisted the ring round and round on his chubby finger. If he thought he had me fascinated, he was right. But I couldn't let him know it. Things were going too fast. After a few puffs, he went on with it.

"I got a special interest in that apartment," he said. "I'm hiring you to look out for it."

I wanted to know more so hard I could taste it, but if I let him go on talking, I'd have one client too many. I figured maybe I had enough information for a start just in the fact that he came to me. So I moved for a quick close. I shook my head hard and definitely.

"I'm not for hire on that case," I said.

He had already got out his wallet and was fingering through the bills. Again he ignored what I'd said.

"I'm giving you five hundred now," he said, "and there's more. I'll send around a key to the apartment, in case you want to look it over."

He threw some bills onto my desk.

"Pick it up," I said. "I'm not with it."

He looked a little surprised then.

"What's wrong with money?" he said.

There was no point in telling him that as between Barney Sorelle and Aaron Krupp, the choice was obvious. I just picked up one of the newspapers, folded it and used it to push his money back to him. It fell off the edge of the desk onto the floor and after staring at me for a minute, he bent over and picked it up. When he straightened he looked sore, but then he laughed, a thin, face-saving kind of laugh, and shrugged his shoulders.

"Well," he said, "that's the first brush-off Barney Sorelle ever got from a cheap keyhole peeper."

You can't make an enemy of a type like Barney Sorelle. That's done for you in advance. So what could I lose?

I walked around the desk and placed my right fist against the left side of his face; not too hard, just hard enough to slap the flabby flesh against his jawbone and send him sprawling on my floor. The cigar flew out of his mouth and his hat fell back off his head. I let him lie there for a minute, staring up at me while he wiggled his jaw carefully, then I picked up his hat and helped him to his feet. He grabbed the hat and shook me off as soon as he was standing.

"Sorelle," I said, "you're what they call an anachronism. You come around here with your loud mouth and your pet gorilla, throwing money at me, and expect me to jump.

"Well, I've got some recent information for you. Those days are gone. There are boys in the rackets around town who could buy you out with their petty cash. They graduated from the nursery to kindergarten. They'll never make high school because they learn too slow. But you haven't got out of the cradle. I wouldn't lift a finger for any of you. There's nothing in it. End of speech. Now run along and talk business with somebody you can hustle."

He went to the door.

"You won't get away with nothing," he said. "Nobody slaps Barney Sorelle."

"I just did," I said.

He went out and I kicked the door shut behind him. I heard him talking to the gorilla outside, but they didn't try to come back in. I heard their footsteps going away and the outer door closing behind them.

I put on my hat, switched the phone over for the call service and left the office. So far, I hadn't accomplished anything except to bother Aaron Krupp at his office, meet Barney Sorelle and make a couple of speeches. In my business, problems are solved with the head and the feet, not the mouth. Maybe I should have lunch. As long as I was shoving food into my mouth, I wouldn't be talking.

CHAPTER 7

I crossed the street to Tony's place. I was finishing off a ham sandwich and a bottle of beer when the front door opened and the *Tribune* reporter who had called earlier in the day walked in, George Keeler. It didn't take him long to find me and we exchanged nods. He slid into the booth across the table from me and ordered a beer for himself. He could pretty well figure on my paying for it.

"I returned your call," I said.

"I know. I checked back."

I ordered a piece of cherry pie because it goes so well with beer.

"I'm sitting on a thing that's pretty hot, Mac," George said, "and I need some advice, maybe some help. I can't sit on it very long."

George was tall and thin and sandy-haired and the only word I can think of for him is nondescript. I know it doesn't mean anything, but when you looked at George, that didn't mean anything either. But he had a mind like a steel trap and you could get your thoughts caught in it before you knew it was there. We got along pretty well because he knew that I knew the trap was there and because I knew that he would shoot square with me if I would return the favor. There were many times when this was difficult, but so far it had worked out all right.

"If it's about that case last night—" I began.

"It is, it is," he said, "but it's a bright new angle. I don't think you know about it."

"I tell you the truth," I said. "I don't know much."

He didn't seem to care what I knew. He had something.

"This thing," he said, "is nothing that will help Donovan solve the case. I think maybe we ought to leave Donovan out of it."

"If it has anything to do with the case, you can't leave Donovan out of it."

"That's why I came to you, pal."

I sighed.

"All right, let's have it."

"We found the girl's father."

I swallowed some beer the wrong way and choked on it. After I got through coughing I had control again.

"Her father?"

"You know—father, padre, sire, daddy—"

"All right. How did you find him? You didn't even know the girl's name."

"He came forward, so to speak. To the office. He wanted the make a statement."

"So. What did he say?"

"He talked quite a while and it began to look like quite a feature for the paper, so I thought I better play it cool. I heard him out and then I bought him an early lunch and sent him home, with a kid from the office to watch over him."

"To protect him from the other papers."

"If you want to put it like that. You can't tell—a guy like that they can crucify."

"You don't say."

I held out my hand, palm up.

"Come on with the rest of it," I said. "What did he say?"

"Well, he's kind of a nut. I figure his story will be good for two or three days, if we handle it right. But we can't fool around with the case, and I couldn't just turn him over to Donovan, because then I'd lose him."

I tried to adopt an attitude of parental sternness.

"George," I said, "you know I can't help you get around Donovan. He's already doing me a couple of favors that draw his neck out. I'd like to help—" George had been gazing at me like a scolded child. Now he gave a little shrug and straightened in his seat as if he were about the leave.

"O. K., Mac," he said. "I just thought that if you could help me along for a couple of hours, so I could get this thing on ice—But I don't want to impose on you."

"I'm sorry," I said.

"It'll be a sensational story. It will be such good copy that I figured it would overshadow anything else that might creep into the news about the case."

He had the trap set. I could feel it. I knew it would snap shut on me any moment, but I couldn't quite find it. I chewed on the last bite of the pie and watched him steadily.

"Such as—" he said slowly, "the fact that the son of a prominent local merchant may be deeply involved. But I can see your point. Forget it, boy."

He slid out of the booth and stood up. I could feel my mind shaking, trying to get out of the trap. I swallowed the last of my beer and got up. He went to the door and I followed. Out in the street he headed for his car.

He got in from the curb side and slid across under the wheel, leaving the door open. I slid in beside him and closed the door.

"It's not far," he said. "The guy's got a room over on North LaSalle. It's handy to Bughouse Square. He spends a lot of time there."

"You son of a bitch," I said.

"Thanks, boy," he said. "Business is business."

We rode for a while.

"It must have been that stupid flatfoot, Robinson," I said.

"He's all right," George said. "He means well, but he ain't real bright."

"I'm glad I'm not in the public-relations business," I said. "You boys play rough."

"It's a rough world."

"It's too bad you weren't around for the Loeb-Leopold case," I said. "You could have been a big help."

"Let's not be bitter, boy," he said.

I gave the round to him and decided to wait for an opening.

CHAPTER 8

We drove slowly along North LaSalle, looking for the number he wanted. The flat, blank walls of cheap apartment buildings lined both sides of the street. The sun was hot now on the street and the few lawns in front of some of the buildings were scraggly and brown. It was too late for winter and too early for spring and the air was heavy with an unnatural heat wave.

George finally stopped and parked the car behind a bakery truck drawn up in front of a delicatessen. I climbed out and followed him into a red brick building. Inside were two rows of mailboxes with dirty, finger-marked cards showing the names of tenants. One of the cards read "Carl Peterson" and George pushed the button under it.

"The girl used the name of Sandor," he explained to me while we waited for a buzzer. "More glamorous, I guess. Girls do that."

"Yeah," I said, "and then lie down on white shag rugs and die."

He looked at me in some surprise.

"I'm glad to know about the white shag rug," he said. "Mind if I make a note of it?"

"You won't have to," I said. "Just string along. Old loose-mouth Mac will feed you everything in due time."

He slapped me on the shoulder.

"You take things so hard, boy," he said.

The buzzer sounded and George opened the vestibule door. We walked into a dim hallway that smelled of onions and stale beer and started up a narrow flight of stairs toward the third floor.

"What kind of a nut is this guy?" I said.

"I'll let you judge for yourself," George said. "I don't mean he's violent or anything."

It was hard to find the room after we got to his floor. The hall was dark and some of the numbers had been scratched over till they were illegible. We finally deduced it by simple arithmetic. George knocked on the door and it opened right away. There was a young man holding it and when he saw George his face lit up like a neon sign.

"Come on in," he said. "Mr. Peterson is waiting. He's been telling me —some things. Very interesting."

I gathered he was a cub reporter who'd got roped in by George and had now had enough of the newspaper business for one day.

"I'd better get on back," he said, edging toward the hall.

"Sure, Jerry," George said. "And stick around my office, will you? I'll be checking in."

The youngster almost ran out the door and down the hall. George chuckled faintly and closed the door.

The room was hot and stuffy and smelled of musty paper. The light that came through the dirty window was gray and dingy. There was a brass bed at one end of the room and a chest of drawers near it. Toward the other end was an overstuffed rocking chair with frayed upholstery and beyond that a screen that partially hid some light-house-keeping equipment. Here and there on the floor were piles of pamphlets and books and some loose papers that had been run through a mimeograph machine. They were covered with a layer of dust.

The man who sat in the chair, watching us as we entered, was tall, thin and cadaverous. He wore a blue work shirt and a pair of dark wool pants held up by white suspenders. He was in his stocking feet and he sat calmly in the chair with his big hands in his lap. Now and then he would rub the back of one hand with the palm of the other and fold his fingers, pressing them to make the knuckles crack. There was a vague, far-off expression in his eyes.

"Hello, Mr. Peterson," George said, introducing me.

The guy nodded without speaking.

"I wanted him to meet you," George went on. "He has an interest in the—tragedy that came to your daughter."

Peterson blinked at him.

"You may call it tragedy, Mr. Keeler," he said, "My daughter lived a sinful life. Inevitably, she was destroyed. There are forces—"

"Yes, yes," George said. "Would you mind telling Mac here what you told me this morning?"

"Could I sit down?" I said.

"Make yourself comfortable."

I backed to the bed and sat down. George came with me. I was developing a hateful attitude toward him and it was hard not to speak of it.

"You were saying, Mr. Peterson—" George urged.

The thin man in the chair moved his head slowly and blinked at the dirty window. I looked at George, who shrugged. Then the guy was talking and I resigned myself to listen.

"The world is evil," he said, "and the day of wrath approaches. No one shall escape; even the good man is evil and rotten unto the core."

I looked at George again, who avoided my eyes. He reached into his pocket absently and pulled out a cigarette. Mr. Peterson gazed at him mournfully.

"Please, Mr. Keeler," he said.

George fumbled the cigarette, dropped it, picked it up and put it back in his pocket.

"Excuse me," he said. "I forgot."

"The people have forgotten," Peterson said, intoning the words. "They forget righteousness and walk in evil ways. Smoking, drinking, committing adultery—surely vengeance will overtake them."

George leaned forward.

"And you say your daughter did all these things?"

I snapped my head around to look at George.

"After all," I said, "the girl is dead—" He made a smoothing-out gesture with his hands. I refrained from gesturing back in an appropriate manner. Peterson went on with his sermon, in a monotone, reciting as if he had learned it all by heart.

"There is no evil like the evil of women. Even unto the third and fourth generation. Though I prayed for them, it availed nothing. Though I wrestled with the evil spirits that lived in them, I wrestled in vain. The day of wrath has overtaken my daughter and surely it will overtake all women, yea, even the most saintly."

He had developed a kind of singsong rhythm. I could have clapped my hands and kept time with him.

"The world must know," he said. "The newspapers must publish it. The radio. The rich and powerful must give aid so that sinfulness will be wiped out and the way of the righteous made plain."

"I see," George said. "And that's why you came to me."

"I came to enlist your paper in the cause of righteousness," he said. "Even though it is vain to struggle, even though the world is infested with evil. My daughter's destruction is less than nothing. The strength of evil is limitless and without end—" I'd had enough.

"Just a minute," I said. "Could I ask a few questions?"

Peterson rubbed the back of his neck and nodded slowly.

"Where was your daughter born?" I asked.

"In a small town downstate," he said. "But this is of no consequence. She began leading a life of sin at an early age—"

"What is the name of the town?" I cut in.

"I beg your pardon?"

I glanced at George and I guess he saw my temper rising, because he got into the conversation quickly.

"Mac here," he said, "is interested in your daughter's death from the—police viewpoint."

Peterson said nothing. I gave up on specific facts and tried another tack.

"When you saw that your daughter was turning to—evil ways," I said, "did you try to help her?"

"As a young man I was blind. I was unaware then of the true nature of evil. Only later did I see the light. Then it was too late."

"Was it too late because your daughter had already left home?"

"It was too late," he repeated.

"When did you learn she had—died?"

He looked at me sadly.

"Young man," he said, "your questions are without meaning. The moment of her worldly end is unimportant. The identity of the agent who brought it about is likewise of no consequence."

"It's of some consequence to the police," I said.

He looked out the window. It made me feel as if I had left the room. I turned to my friend, the reporter.

"George," I said, "the hell with it."

I got up and adjusted my hat. George got up with me.

"Thank you, Mr. Peterson," he said, "for giving us this time. I'd like to check with you after I've written the story." Peterson nodded, but said nothing. I was already out the door. George came along, closing it behind him and we started down the stairs toward the street. Light footsteps sounded below, approaching hesitantly up the stairs. A girl reached the landing, started up toward us and George and I flattened against the wall to let her pass. She went a couple of steps, then stopped. I turned to look at her. She was a very pretty girl, very young, smartly dressed and she carried a small slip of paper in one hand.

"Excuse me," she said. "I'm looking for a—Carl Peterson."

I started to point the way, then held my hand back.

"Sure you have the right address?" I said.

She looked at her paper, read the address aloud.

"I think it's right," she said. "I'm a stranger in town."

"Mr. Peterson's a relative of yours?" I asked, trying to sound neighborly.

"No," she said. "It's about a job."

I nodded sadly.

"It's tough looking for work," I said. "You're a stenographer?"

"No. A model—" Suddenly her manner changed from frank, unquestioning trust to frank, hostile suspicion—as it should have.

"Why all the questions?" she said. "I'm just looking—"

I pointed on up the stairs.

"I didn't mean to be nosy," I said. "Mr. Peterson is on the fourth floor. Room four-o-nine."

"Thank you," she said curtly, turned away and disappeared upward.

I stood there for a minute, then went on down, following George who had gone ahead. In the vestibule he yanked a cigarette from his pocket and lit it jerkily.

"Please, Mr. Keeler," I said.

"Shut up."

We got in the car and he stalled it twice before we got away. I kept quiet till he got going and then I said, "That's a hell of a story you've got."

"It'll do," he said, "until another one comes along."

We were driving down Chicago Avenue toward Michigan and I let him sweat over it for a while.

"If I give you a good one, will you leave me alone?" I asked.

He put a clamp on his curiosity and looked at me with a stony stare.

"I'll try it on for size," he said.

"All I can give you is the lead. You'll have to dig the rest out for yourself."

"I suppose it's all right for you to tell me?"

"Barney Sorelle tried to hire me to investigate the case," I said. "He's got a key to that apartment."

He stopped the car where it was, in the middle of the street, and looked at me—for a long time.

"Now who's a son of a bitch?" he said; "you bastard."

I opened the car door.

"O. K.," I said. "Some guys don't appreciate anything."

"Come on back," he said. "Why did you let me go through all that routine with that nut, Peterson? You just trying to stall on the Sorelle angle till all the others have it in the composing room?"

"Relax," I said, "there hasn't been time for anybody else to get it."

At Michigan he had to stop for a light.

"Could I drop you here, Mac?" he said. "I've got to get to the office."

"Sure," I said. "Thanks for the free entertainment."

He'd forgotten about me. He just wanted to get on with it. He was framing the story with his lips as he waited for the light to change while I climbed out.

"What a yarn," he said aloud, "if Barney Sorelle should get religion—with the help of Carl Peterson."

I slammed the door shut.

"I'll be waiting for the early edition," I said.

44

I don't think George heard me.

I went into the drugstore on the corner and looked under PHOTOGRA-PHERS—COMMERCIAL, in the phone directory. I found Ben Cham-plain listed at an address on the northwest side. I memorized the street number and closed the book. I went around the corner to the office and got in my car. I'd left the window down on the curb side and before I could get into gear, there was a hand on the sill and a guy's head looking in at me. Sound came out of it.

"Hey, bud."

It was half whisper, half croak.

CHAPTER 9

The face looked old as ancient parchment, pinched and thin, with sharp features and that look in the eyes that comes when joy is gone and desperation has settled in for keeps. It was in some need of a shave and there was a noticeable tic in the left eyebrow. I did not recognize any part of it. Also, I could not estimate its age. It might have been forty or it might have been a hundred.

"The name is Mac, not Bud," I said.

He nodded.

"I know. I see in the papers you was mixed up in that killin' last night."

"Not exactly," I said.

There was a faraway look in his eyes.

"That was Miss Sandor's apartment," he said dreamily. "I was there once."

He said it as if he were reporting a visit to Valhalla.

"Recently?" I asked politely.

He forced his attention back to me reluctantly.

"Some time ago," he said. "I thought maybe there might be somethin' I could tell you—"

"How much will it cost?"

His eyes dropped and rose again.

"I ain't here to hold you up, Mac," he said. "But ever since the place shut down, I been in a bad way."

"What place?"

He looked surprised.

"The dress shop," he said. "Miss Sandor's place."

"Miss Sandor was in the dress business?"

"Oh yeh."

My clenched hand slipped a little on the wheel.

"And you worked there?"

He got the dreamy look again.

"Three years," he said.

I reached across the seat and flipped the door open.

"Want to get in?" I said. "I've got a call to make. We can talk on the way."

46

...ed the door open and got in.

...said. "I got nothin' else much to do."

...e street.

...our name?" I asked.

...ard Jones," he said. "Around the place, they used to call me ...ie.'"

It pleased him to remember the nickname.

"What did you do there?"

"Oh I wasn't nobody much. I done a little of everything. Kind of a handy man, you know?"

"You didn't help make the dresses?"

"Oh no. Mostly women done that. Two, three men—but they was cutters."

"Did you work directly for Miss Sandor?"

"I was in and out of her office all the time. Used to tidy it up in the mornin'. She always had a smile for me..." His faded eyes went rapt again. "'Good morning, Howie,' she'd say. Every time. Never failed."

"You liked Miss Sandor all right then?"

He turned his head and I could feel the earnest light coming out of his eyes.

"I tell you, Mac, I would have walked through fire for that girl. Through fire!"

"Then I doubt that she would have asked it of you."

"I tell you," he said, and choked a little, "I wish it had been me that had got killed in her place."

I slowed the car, mapping a route in my mind that would lead to Ben Champlain's studio.

"When did the place shut down?" I asked.

"'Bout a year ago," he said. "I couldn't believe it when I heard—Miss Sandor told me herself."

He paused, overcome by the pain of the memory, and I prompted him.

"It was early one mornin', I went in to clean up her office, and there she was, settin' at her desk. But not doin' nothin'—just kind of starin'.

"'Mornin', Miss Sandor,' I says, 'will it be all right to clean up now?' Because I usually got done by the time she come in, only this time she come so early.

"And she says, 'Certainly, Howie; how are you today?' and gives me that smile, like always. But not quite. I see she was troubled. But I didn't say nothin', just went to work. And pretty soon she told me.

"'Howie,' she says, 'we're closing down.' I couldn't believe it. I just looked at her. 'It's no good any more,' she says, kind of spreadin' her

47

hands. 'I'm not working for myself any more. Everything is for some
else. I'm not even me any more.'"

"How was that?" I asked.

"That's what she said. And some more, but I can't remember it all.
When I got done tidyin' up, she says, 'I'll see you get two weeks' pay,
Howie, and maybe I can get you another job.' But I didn't care about that.
All I wanted was to work for her."

"Did she get you another job?"

"She did. But nothin' was ever the same again. It was a porter's job in
a nightclub. Place called the House of Jazz. I quit after while. Then it
seemed like I couldn't get nothin' else."

"And the only reason she gave for closing down was what she told
you?"

"That's all. But I don't think that was the reason at all."

"You don't?"

"Because—one day I found somethin'."

He dug into his inner coat pocket and brought out a frayed wallet. I
saw that his fingers were stiff and clumsy as he searched through it and
found a cracked, finger-smudged square of stiff, white paper. He handed it
to me and I pulled in to the curb and stopped the car.

It was a photoprint, an eight by ten, that had originally been crumpled,
later smoothed out and folded twice. As I opened it, carefully to minimize
the cracking, I saw there was a hole in it the size of a quarter.

"It was in her wastebasket," he said. "I kept it."

The crumpling and folding had reduced the surface of the print to
something resembling a worn-out fresco, but I made out the general out-
line. It was a photograph of a nude girl lying on a white shag rug, and the
hole was where the head would have been, if it had not been cut out.
There was no way to tell whether it was a good photo or a bad one—and
there was no way to be certain about the white shag rug. But the auto-
graph, slanting across one corner in a bold, black hand, was clear enough.
It read: *Marta Sandor.*

Howie spoke again.

"Ain't that a dirty way to treat a fine girl like Miss Sandor? I tell you—
I like to died when I seen that."

There was nothing to be gained by staring at the picture, so I handed it
back to him. I wanted to keep it, but I couldn't ask him for all he had left
of a woman he'd worshipped.

"Did you cut the face out?" I said.

"No. It was like that when I found it—all crumpled up, layin' in the
basket."

I got the car started again and prowled the streets slowly, looking for the number I had in mind.

"Then it's your theory, Howie," I said, "that some low-down skunk planted this picture of Miss Sandor and she felt so bad about it that she closed down her business?"

He blew his top. I ducked and slowed the car as he swung around in his seat.

"That ain't no kind of thing to say! Miss Sandor would never of posed for any such picture as that. If you'd knowed her, you'd know she wouldn't."

"I'm sorry," I said. "It had her name on it. I took it for granted."

"Maybe it had her name on it. But you can write any name on a picture. That's why the head was cut out—so she'd think it was somebody that looked like her."

"Oh."

He calmed down some and spoke in a confidential tone.

"My theory," he said, "is that whoever done this was blackmailin' Miss Sandor. And that's why she said she was workin' for somebody else. You know why I think so?"

"No. Why?"

"Because after I went to work at that club, the House of Jazz, I seen a whole stack of them pictures, with Miss Sandor's name on 'em."

"Was there a hole where the head should have been?"

"No. There wasn't no holes."

"And it was not Miss Sandor's face?"

"No. This was some girl with dark hair."

I turned a corner slowly.

"Miss Sandor was a blonde?"

"Yellow-haired, pretty as a picture—a decent picture."

I thought, but refrained from saying, how the color of a girl's hair can be changed and how a man sees what he wants to see, whether it's real or not. But except for that reservation, I had to admit that Howie's theory was as good as any that had turned up so far.

I was crawling along, close to the curb, looking for the number. It was an area of industrial shops and warehouses, and trucks lined both sides of the street and rumbled out of alleys. There were no empty parking spaces. I guess Howie hadn't been paying much attention to our route, because he leaned forward suddenly, nearly bumping his head on the windshield, and said, "There it is! The old place. Miss Sandor's place. We're right in front of it!"

I stopped and looked out. There was no sign on the high brick building, which looked now like a warehouse, with boarded-up windows, the front entrance a litter of refuse.

"This is where the dress company was?" I said.

"That's it, Mac."

I glanced at the place next door, a low building with a glass brick front. There was a sign over the door, reading:

BEN CHAMPLAIN—PHOTOGRAPHER

The near side of the studio butted up flush against the wall of the warehouse, but on the far side was a narrow drive with a sign over it reading: PARKING IN REAR.

"If you want to wait," I said, "I'll take you wherever you want to go. If you don't want to wait, I'll give you enough money now so you can take a taxi."

He scratched the back of his neck with long, dry fingers.

"If it's all the same to you," he said, "I don't feel so good hangin' around this neighborhood."

I got out my wallet and gave him two tens and a five.

"You've been a help to me," I told him. "Will you give me your address, so I can get in touch with you later?"

He thought it over.

"Thanks, Mac," he said. "Yeah, I'll give you my address." He mentioned a street and number not far away. "A roomin' house," he said. "This will pay my back rent and buy a few groceries."

"Good," I said.

He climbed out of the car and shut the door. Then he leaned in through the open window.

"Look—" he said, "you won't have to mention my name, will you? See—I didn't exactly quit that job at the House of Jazz. I got fired—because I found them pictures—and raised hell. So they fired me."

"I won't use your name," I said.

He clung to the window sill.

"After I quit—got fired—they was a couple of tough mugs used to come around, tellin' me to keep my mouth shut about the pictures. I was scared at first—moved a couple of times. But I got over it. What the hell —I got nothin' more to lose."

"Take it easy, Howie," I said. "If you have any trouble, give me a ring."

"O. K, Mac," he said.

He pushed away from the car, straightening somewhat. I was his friend now and it made him feel better. Still, I would never be able to replace Marta Sandor.

He walked away, stumbling a little as his feet felt for the curb, and I turned into the alley beside Ben Champlain's studio.

CHAPTER 10

The studio building ended short of the rear of the old Marta Sandor factory and there was a paved parking area with white-bordered spaces facing into the warehouse wall. I found a vacant one, parked and got out.

The back entrance was a heavy steel door with a big knob. I pushed it open and stepped into a corridor that ran through the building to the front, on the warehouse side. The walls on both sides were rough brick and there were heavy doors set into them, one on my right marked "Lab—Do Not Enter." Halfway along the left wall toward the front was a double door of steel with a complicated latching system of bars and cleats. It would probably lead into the warehouse next door.

I met no one in the corridor and at its end came to a glass paneled door marked "Office." In the office was a girl in a sweater and long, stringy hair. She looked at me without expression from a cubicle beyond a waist-high rail with a swinging gate.

"Mr. Champlain?" I said.

"He's in the lab," she said.

"Could he come out of the lab long enough to talk to me?"

"May I tell him who's calling?"

"What if I'm a customer?"

She was temporarily at a loss. Her hands fluttered.

"I might want to buy some pictures," I said.

That made it easier for her. She pushed a button on a cheap intercom system and said, "Mr. Champlain—there's a gentleman out front...O. K." To me she said, "Will you sit down, please?"

I sat in a chair against the wall and looked at the girl in the sweater for a while, then at the ceiling, finally at the floor. And by that time, Ben Champlain had made it from the lab to the office.

He was middle-aged, balding, thick-set and muscular. He wore a light-weight T-shirt and a pair of faded blue slacks. He came up, took a look at me and stopped dead. I got out of the chair.

"Mr. Champlain?" I said.

He examined me with bitterness.

"Haven't you guys had enough yet?" he said.

"You—guys?" I said.

He found a twisted cigarette, stuck it in his mouth and lit it. He had to strike three matches to get it done.

"You cops!" he said, spitting on his own floor.

I decided that either he was cop-happy or I was losing my plain but inoffensive appearance. It frightened me briefly, but I got a grip on myself and played it straight. It never really works to beat around the bush. I gave Champlain my card. He glanced at it and tossed it over the rail toward the receptionist.

"All right—a *private* cop," he said. "What's your beef?"

"No beef—yet. You want to talk here?"

He glanced toward the girl.

"Phyllis!" he barked. "Take a break."

She jumped up as if somebody had pinched her and came skittering out through the swinging gate. She went out the front door to the street. Champlain waited till she was gone, then said, "Well?"

"A girl has died recently," I said, "in an apartment on Walton Place. She had two names: Marta Sandor and Diana Peterson. In the apartment there was a classified telephone directory. Two names in it were marked with a pencil. One was mine, the other was yours. Why?"

The bent cigarette flopped in his mouth. He had sharp black eyes and they crawled over me like flies.

"What else?" he said.

"Nothing else. The girl is dead. Here I am."

He swung away from me, ploughed through the gate and started beating on the rail with his clenched fist.

"The dirty little tramp," he said, "trying to drag me into it—"

"Into what?"

"Ahh—!"

"Besides, it's not polite to speak roughly of the dead. They can't defend themselves."

He went on beating his fist on the rail.

"The dirty little tramp!" he said.

I sat down again.

"When you get through beating yourself," I said, "let's talk it over."

He quit the hammering but went on glaring. I tried to give him some confidence.

"The cops aren't through," I said. "They'll pick you up and sweat you. Maybe I could help."

"I don't think I can afford your rates."

"It's not money I came for. It's information."

He went on glaring for a while, then slumped all over and sat down on the edge of a chair with his head in his hands. Finally he looked up.

"All right," he said dully. "What do you want to know?"

He acted like a man with plenty on his mind and most of it unwelcome. I wondered how far out of bounds he had strayed.

"How long did you know this Marta Sandor?" I said.

He shrugged.

"Less than two years."

"That was in a business way?"

"Sure. She modeled some."

"Clothes?"

"Clothes—yeah."

"Her own?"

"Sometimes—what do you mean, 'her own'?"

"I understand she manufactured dresses at one time."

"That chick?" He laughed, very sardonic. Then he shrugged. "Maybe. I wouldn't know."

"Besides the clothes—did she model anything else? Like white shag rugs?"

His eyes narrowed and he tightened up.

"Now look, bud—"

"The name is Mac. I asked the question because you referred to her as a 'dirty little tramp,' and also because I saw a picture recently of a girl on a white shag rug and it might have been Marta Sandor. The cops have some pictures of her now in practically the same position. But the one I saw was made some time ago."

"I couldn't tell without seeing it."

"Why did you call her a 'dirty little tramp'?"

"So I'm not a gentleman!"

"Take it easy. What can you tell me about her? Where did she come from?"

His patience had run out. He got to his feet, ending the interview.

"I don't know, see? She was nobody from nowhere. She was a tramp and I took some pictures of her. All my relations with her were strictly business. Does that answer your questions?"

I climbed to my own feet.

"Not altogether," I said. "Do you have any idea why she might have called me? Was she afraid of something?"

"She was always afraid of something. Always in a trap."

"What kind?"

"She set 'em for herself. She was—she was a nothing! She didn't like it. She wanted to be somebody else."

"Do you know her father?"

"I heard she had one."

I studied him for a moment.

"O. K.," I said, "one more. What makes you so upset?"

His nerves were on a thin edge and I watched the struggle he made to keep from blowing up. His voice was low and tight.

"Look," he said, "I work for a living. I work hard. Three times today I've been interrupted by cops and private eyes asking questions—"

"Three times?"

"Two sets of cops—then you."

"I know Lieutenant Donovan was here, maybe with an assistant. But who made up the other set?"

"One guy—some stupid flatfoot."

"Name of Robinson?"

"How would I know his name? Just another cop. Big man! Talked real tough."

I started off toward the rear exit, Champlain following me.

"All right," I said. "Maybe I won't have to bother you again."

At the double door in the warehouse wall I paused and rattled the heavy fastenings.

"This lead next door?" I asked. "I hear that's where Miss Sandor used to have her dress business."

He shrugged at me.

"I've only been in this studio six months. There's a warehouse—I don't know what's in it."

"Do you know who owns it?"

"How would I know?"

We went on past the door, three or four paces, and I heard it opening behind us. I stopped, turning back and Champlain had to sidestep to avoid bumping me.

Half of the big door had opened a foot or so and a guy was looking out at me.

"What's goin' on?" he said.

He was the ex-pug, the one who had been with Barney Sorelle at my office earlier in the day. He looked at me and the light of recognition dawned slowly in his eyes.

"That's the one," he said slowly, then looked back over his shoulder. "He slugged Barney."

Somebody behind him grunted an answer. The door opened farther and two of them came out into the corridor. Beside me, Ben Champlain cursed under his breath. I was trying to see beyond the two heavyweights into the warehouse, but they managed to block the view. The second one was bigger than the one I remembered, but, if possible, even slower to react. They

54

were like two throwbacks to a primitive era and therefore somewhat fascinating.

They advanced slowly, staring at me, and I had an impulse to laugh but restrained it. A laugh would bring them on faster and there really wasn't much of anywhere for me to go.

Champlain spoke up suddenly.

"Where did *you* come from?" he asked.

The leader stopped and looked at him in some bewilderment.

"You know where we come from," he said.

He waited for his companion to come alongside. The scene resembled the maneuvering of a couple of tugboats. When they got into position they gave me a mutually stolid stare and finally the talkative one found some more words.

"Some bright boys think they can get away with anything," he said. "I think we better learn this one different—huh, Alex?"

"Yeah," Alex said.

"Hallelujah!" I said and turned my back on them.

I walked away with my ears open. Sure enough, they started after me and I swung back, looking for a hole between them.

But the only thing between them was the photographer, Champlain, with a hand each on their manly chests.

"You nuts or something?" he said. "Relax!"

The one with all the words gave him an injured look.

"But, Ben! He slugged Barney!"

"So what?" Ben said, holding them.

But I knew he couldn't have held them without some moral authority, the source of which I couldn't know.

"Good-bye, Mr. Champlain," I said. "You have my card."

Mr. Champlain didn't answer. I went on quickly, got in my car and headed for the Loop.

CHAPTER 11

I had to wait fifteen minutes in Aaron Krupp's outer office. When I finally got in, he apologized. His office was high-ceilinged and comfortable, on the tenth floor of his downtown store. He offered me a cigar, which I declined. He sat at a wide, cleared desk and I stood across the desk from where he sat.

"Well, Mac?" he said.

"Marta Sandor," I said, "at one time manufactured dresses. I figure you would know more about this than I would."

He looked at me out of his wide, quiet face behind a cloud of cigar smoke. After a minute, he got up from his chair, took my arm and ushered me through a side door into a private elevator. He pushed a button and we started down.

"There's a lot in the store," he said, "that if you would ask me, I wouldn't know what it was."

"It's a big store," I said.

"But in ladies' ready-to-wear, I know my way around."

Then there's something you know that I don't, I thought, but I didn't say so. I forget what I said.

We stepped out of the elevator on the third floor and walked down a long corridor toward the rear of the building. There was a wide door with no sign on it and Aaron Krupp pushed it open.

It was big inside, a stockroom, and it was full of nothing but dresses— row after row of racks, packed with hangers, from each of which hung a dress. There may have been some blouses among them, but they all looked like dresses to me.

I followed Mr. Krupp along an aisle between two rows of the portable racks until he stopped finally. I waited patiently and he reached into the tight-packed rack, got hold of a dress and pulled it out into the aisle.

I looked at it, then at him.

"Looks like a nice dress," I said. "Hard to tell without seeing it on a live form."

He smiled a little, shook the dress off the hanger and threw it at me. I caught it.

"Look at the label," he said.

56

I fumbled for the place at the back of the neck where the label would be. It was a lavender rectangle with the name of the manufacturer lettered in gold across it. The name was "Marta Sandor."

I looked at Aaron Krupp and tossed the dress back to him. He caught it and replaced it on the rack.

"Was it a good line?" I asked.

He shrugged.

"It moved all right. We took it off the floor to start something else. After a while we'll put these back."

"They ought to move real good when Donovan lets that name get into the papers. Either real good or not at all."

He led me out of the stockroom, down the hall and back into the elevator. As we started up he said, "The girl who died did not make the dresses."

I followed him back into his office.

"Well," I said, "do you know the girl who did make the dresses?"

He turned from me slowly, moved to the wide window beyond his desk and stood with his hands clasped behind his back.

"Yes," he said. "I knew her."

"A long time?"

He shrugged.

"A couple of years."

"You knew her as 'Marta Sandor'?"

"That's right."

"And she was not the girl who was found dead in the apartment on Walton Place?"

"No. That is another girl."

I took off my hat, scratched my head and replaced the hat. It made me think of Donovan.

Easy, Mac, I thought.

"You must have known that this morning," I said, "when we rode downtown."

"I thought so. I wasn't positive."

"Would it be all right for me to ask how you got to be positive?"

"Certainly." He turned from the window and he was smiling. "I don't try to hide anything, Mac. No description in the paper. Norman was upset, maybe couldn't remember so good. I called him a while ago. He told me it was the girl he was going with. So I knew it wasn't Marta Sandor."

He sat down at his desk, indicated a chair for me. I sat down and took off my hat. I started to scratch my head again, then refrained.

"When did you last see this Marta Sandor?" I asked. "The one who made the dresses?"

He tipped back in his chair, closed his eyes.

"Seven, eight months ago," he said. "The business shut down and she went away. Somewhere. I lost touch with her."

"But before that—you knew her quite well?"

"In a way, yes. In another way, no."

I didn't like the way I was having to pull this out of him. I guess it showed in my face, because he came forward in his chair, leaning on the desk, and looked at me frankly.

"Marta Sandor was a charming girl, a very smart designer, plenty of talent. She came to me with samples. They were good. I tried to help her."

"By taking on the line?"

"In different ways. Taking on the line—sure."

He lit another cigar, puffed on it slowly.

"You try to help people, Mac—sometimes it works, sometimes not. Some people ain't worth it. This girl was worth it. Every minute."

There was a big load of conviction in his voice.

"I would have told you about her. Believe me, there's nothing to hide. But if the thing can be solved—the death of Norman's girl—without bothering Marta Sandor, that would be better. I wouldn't want to see her dragged in."

I looked at him. No matter how objectively I looked, I couldn't see him as a guy to play around. He talked about this Marta Sandor the way a man talks about a niece or a daughter. So I would take his word for it, until I had reason not to.

"Maybe she won't have to come into it," I said. "Do you know where she is?"

"No. I think she planned to go out West."

"Did her dress business fold up? Why did it shut down?"

"I don't think it folded. She never told me where the financing came from. It takes capital."

"But you think she was in the black when she quit?"

"I think so. Can't know for sure."

"This other girl—the dead one—you said you met her once."

"That's right."

"And she was using the name Marta Sandor?"

"Yes. She also claimed to have made the dresses. I already knew better. But even if I never knew the other girl—I've been in this business all my life. If a girl makes dresses, she knows how to say so. Norman's girl didn't."

"But you didn't expose her."

"For the boy's sake. What good would it do?"

I stood up and put my hat on.

"I'd like to talk to Norman this afternoon," I said. "Where would I find him?"

He didn't hesitate.

"By the laboratory," he said. "This is the long day. He fiddles with the test tubes."

"Will they let him go out for a talk?"

The old man chuckled.

"He ain't in jail, Mac. It's a school."

"Thanks," I said.

Going out, I was a little self-conscious. I'd never gone to school much.

* * * *

In a phone booth on the store's main floor I dialed a girl named Dottie Ellender. Dottie's business was looking things up—practically anything that could be looked up, statistical, political, economic—the works. She was good at it and I had used her from time to time. When I told her I had a job for her, she said, "O. K., Dreamboat, who you fingering this time?"

"Outfit used to make dresses," I said. "Here in town. D B A Marta Sandor. Find out who paid the bills, whether they made money or lost it. Get the names of the owner, or owners."

"When did it start?"

"Something over three years ago."

"Confidential?" she said.

"More or less."

"I'll call you," she said and hung up.

I left the store and hiked to the lot where I'd parked the car.

CHAPTER 12

It was an off hour for traffic, so it only took half an hour to get out to the University and find a parking place a couple of blocks from the east end of the campus. Then I had to walk half a mile or more to find the science quadrangle and the lab where Mr. Krupp had told me I would find Norman.

The sun was shining and students were walking around carrying books, or sitting in couples and groups, talking. I overheard snatches of the conversations and some of it was ordinary small talk. But some of it was another language, and I found myself thinking.

What if I'd gone to school like these kids, instead of trying to beat my way to somewhere with my hands?

I began to feel old and used-up and pretty soon I thought, If I had done this, I wouldn't have known Donovan. I wouldn't have got the education he gave me. I would have got some other kind and maybe it would have been better. But it was all past now. There was nothing in looking back.

Still, I thought, I wonder how many of these kids would have to wake in the night and remember the desperate, twisted faces of men and women who needed help and couldn't go to the police; remember the hard, nervous hands of the professional sadists, or the dead, beautiful face of a nude girl on a white shag rug.

One of them, Norman Krupp, would remember that last. But even for him, it was only one. If he had any luck at all, he wouldn't have them stacked up on him.

Then, in the middle of these thoughts, a girl came along the walk toward me. She was pretty and healthy looking and she had an armful of notebooks and papers that I couldn't see how she could carry. She smiled at me and nodded.

"Hi!" she said.

"Hello," I said and went on.

I felt fine again.

I found Norman Krupp sitting on a bench in a corner of the lab, wearing a white smock, gazing at a row of test tubes in a little rack. There were different colored liquids in them. As I came closer, I saw that he was just staring at them. His face was full of pain. There weren't many others in the lab and they were at some distance.

I walked up to him slowly, approaching from the front so he would notice me coming. I watched him pull himself together when he recognized me. He nodded, but there was no smile on his face.

"How's it coming?" I said, pointing to the tubes.

He shrugged and stood up away from the bench.

"I don't know," he said. "It's all in the book anyway. I had to have something to do."

"Could we go somewhere for a while?" I said.

He studied my face.

"I'd just as soon not talk about it," he said.

"There are some things I have to know. It would be good to got them over with."

"Are you working for the Lieutenant?"

"No."

"Who then?"

"Well, in a way, for you."

"I didn't ask for help."

"I know."

"Was it my father?"

With a kid like him, you couldn't spin yarns.

"I told him I'd look into the thing," I said. "To tell you the truth, I don't know whether I can do any good or not."

"Why do you bother?" he said. "She's dead. What difference does it make now?"

I knew how he felt. The girl was dead and he might as well be dead himself. That feeling would pass, but he felt it strongly now. I was no psychiatrist. I had neither the time nor the talent to straighten him out where he really lived. I had to use tricks.

"One difference it might make," I said, "is with the newspapers. Whenever a beautiful girl gets murdered, the reporters get very busy—"

"I don't care what they say about me," he said. "It doesn't matter anymore."

"I wasn't thinking of you. I was thinking of what they'll say about her. After all, she can't very well sue for libel."

It was a little like hitting him in the stomach, but it worked. He began to take off the smock. I went on, trying to wrap it up.

"The reporters will play along," I said, "if they get the straight dope from a source they can trust. The more they have to speculate, the rougher it gets."

"Where do you want to go?" he said.

"I don't care. Outside—anywhere."

He put on a suede jacket and arranged some papers on the bench beside the test tubes. We crossed the lab and stepped outside. The quadrangle was pretty well filled and he said, "Over on the Midway?"

"Sure."

We came out of the campus onto 59th Street and crossed to the Midway. I found an isolated spot and we sat down on the grass. Young Krupp leaned on an elbow and plucked grass by the handful, throwing it away after he'd looked at it.

"Where did you meet this girl?" I said.

"Marta? At a party…"

He'd gone with some friends to this bohemian party at an apartment on the Near North Side—not far from my office. The girl had been there, unescorted, and he'd fallen like the side of a mountain. It would be hard to imagine anybody more susceptible. She was glamorous, she modeled, she was awfully easy to look at, and she was so friendly. I couldn't help cringing as he spun out the pattern.

One thing led to another and he thought it was all his own doing. She'd tried to hold him off at first, in his own interest, but then began to give in. Finally she'd agreed to see him once a week. Since he had to study so much, it wouldn't be fair to him to take up his time. She couldn't bring herself to stand in the way of his success.

At first on their weekly dates, they'd gone out to the hotels and nightclubs, theater, always somewhere. Then they began staying in the apartment. She hadn't given him the key until the last date they'd had, the week before. Their weekly date was always on Friday—never any other day. He hadn't asked for the key, she'd thought of it herself and offered it to him. He was a little frightened about it, but he took it.

Then, when he had it, he began to feel more sure of himself. He wasn't supposed to see her, even to call her, until the next Friday. But he couldn't wait. He spent a lot of time torturing himself, wondering what she did on the nights he didn't see her, and it was as much an imaginative kind of jealousy as anything else that made him go to the apartment on Thursday, the night before this day when we sat on the Midway, talking.

He kept telling himself he shouldn't do it, that he would be breaking faith with her. Also, he was a little scared about what he might find if he let himself in. He had to work on it for a couple of hours before he could get up the nerve to go ahead. He went first at about ten-thirty. The apartment was empty and dark. He sat in the dark for a while, waiting, then decided he couldn't stand it to be sitting there if she came home with some other guy, so he let himself out.

By this time his anxiety was so big he couldn't give up. He wandered around the streets near the place, waiting for her to come home. He was afraid to loiter too close to the building in that neighborhood, so he stuck around the corner of Chicago and Michigan most of the time.

Finally, at one o'clock in the morning, he walked past the building and saw lights in her windows. He used his key and went in, thinking he'd surprise her. He'd listened at the door long enough to make sure there was nobody with her. For a while he thought she wasn't there herself, but he could see the light under the door.

"It was awful," he said, burying his face for a moment in his hands. "She was lying there, on the rug. The rug was twisted and rumpled, as if somebody had run and slipped on it. I thought that's what had happened, that she'd fainted or something. I got a washcloth from the bathroom and soaked it and tried to bring her around. I rubbed her arms and face. But it didn't do any good."

He choked on it. I waited.

"Finally it soaked in," he said, "she was either dead or too sick for me to help her. I straightened out the rug and called the police."

"You straightened out the rug?"

"I don't know why—it just didn't look right for her to be lying that way on a rumpled carpet—"

"Was there any other disorder in the room?"

"I don't know—there was a pillow on the floor."

"A pillow."

"I picked it up and put it back where it belonged, on the davenport."

I wasn't feeling very good.

"Was there anything else lying around? Anything at all? Did you touch anything else?"

"There was a highball glass. It had got turned over, but I guess it must have been empty. Nothing ran out of it onto the rug."

"That was near the girl somewhere?"

"It was on the rug."

"What did you do with that?"

"I picked it up and took it to the kitchen."

"And put it on the shelf?"

"Yes. There was a bottle of whisky on the shelf—almost full."

"And you wiped all your fingerprints off?"

"What?"

"Nothing."

Isn't it a beautiful day? I thought. Isn't it one hell of a beautiful, lovely day?

"I wasn't thinking about those things," he said.

63

"All right. What did you do after you called the police?"

"I just sat there."

"Where did you sit?"

"On the davenport." Then he looked at my eyes. "What difference does it make?"

"Not much. I'm trying to get a picture."

We sat there for a while and then I said, "You knew of course that 'Marta Sandor' was not her real name."

"No I did not know it. Anyway, what's in a name?"

"Maybe murder's in it," I said. "Didn't you know that your father's store carries a line of dresses made by Marta Sandor?"

He shrugged.

"I haven't paid much attention to the store for a long time."

"But you did know that the girl you were going with did not make dresses."

"I never heard about it."

After a minute, I said, "There's a guy named Peterson," I said, "who claims to be her father."

He shot me a fast look, then gazed out across the Midway.

"Where did you find him?" he asked.

"One of the newspapers found him."

There was some more silence.

"He was some kind of fanatic," Norman said.

"Why did you tell me she had no kin? Why did you want to claim her body yourself?"

"He wasn't her real father."

"Well, what was the connection?"

"I don't know. He was somebody she knew when she first came to Chicago. She used to laugh about him. She said he was always trying to save her soul."

"Did her soul need saving?"

Anger reddened his face.

"You keep making insinuations," he said.

"Try to keep calm. Speaking of money, do you have any idea where she got enough to maintain an apartment like that? Was she working?"

"She worked sometimes, modeling. She got good fees."

"I don't doubt it. Still—" He got to his feet. He'd had enough. No matter how long I might keep him there now, it wouldn't do any good to ask him any more questions.

"There you go again!" he said. "Prying, suspicious—what good will it do, now she's dead? Why can't you at least leave her memory alone?"

"I'd like to," I said. "But I've got a job—"

"A hell of a way to earn a living!"

"It sure is." I got up and brushed off my clothes. "By the way, do you still have the key to her apartment?"

"Maybe I have," he said, challenging me. "What are you going to do? Go back there and snoop around?"

I held onto myself. I could get pretty hot myself if he kept after me and that wouldn't help any. I kept telling myself that he hadn't hired me, that he hadn't asked for anything. I knew what I was doing right now wasn't much help to him, that it was just something I had to do.

"You can give it any name you want to," I said. "I have to go in there and take a look. I'll get in all right, one way or another, but it would make it easier if you'd lend me your key."

He looked past me, beyond my shoulder, and his lips moved with the struggle he was going through. Then he reached into his pocket and pulled out a key. He handed it to me and I put it in my own pocket.

"Shall we walk back to the campus?" I said.

We didn't speak till we got to the entrance to his quadrangle on 59th Street. There weren't any words in my head that could help him now. He started off toward the campus and I said.

"One more thing, if you've got a minute."

He stopped.

"Yes?"

"Did you ever hear Marta mention Barney Sorelle?"

He looked disgusted.

"That hoodlum?"

"That hoodlum."

"How would she know him?"

It was a logical answer, for a kid in his condition, but it was an evasion too. I decided not to press the point now. I figured I'd put him through enough for one session.

"O. K., and thanks," I said. "If you want to talk to me, my number's in the book. I've got a call service."

"All right," he said, "but I don't imagine I'll want to talk to you."

"So long," I said and walked away to where I had parked my car.

It seemed to me I'd learned something from him. I couldn't be sure, but it seemed to me that he had begun to worry about the girl, and how he stood. He had begun to have doubts about her and maybe these doubts were bothering him almost as much as her death. The big question was— when did he begin to have those doubts and how strong were they? Were they strong enough to set him off? And if so—when?

A big question—and dangerous. When? Before her death? Or after it?

It was four in the afternoon and I stopped at a drugstore, went into a phone booth and called Aaron Krupp at his office.

"I just talked to Norman," I said. "I don't know why the police haven't bothered him yet, but I think they will get around to it. They may pick him up and take him downtown."

There was a pause and then his deep, calm voice.

"Well, Mac?"

"Do you have a lawyer on retainer?"

"Yes."

"I would call him and ask him to stand by. Then if Norman is picked up, you should let the lawyer know right away, in time for him to meet the cops when they bring the boy in. If your own lawyer is tied up, you had better get another one."

"All right, Mac. Anything else?"

"No. The attorney will know what to do."

"I'm calling him right now," he said.

"I'll check with you later," I said and hung up.

* * * *

When I opened my office door, I found a piece of white scratch paper that had been slid under it. There was a hastily written message.

"Mac: Thanks for the lead. I guess it's hot all right. But so is Barney Sorelle. Watch your step, boy." It was signed, "George."

I threw the note in the wastebasket and went to bed to get a couple of hours' sleep. But the telephone rang and kept on ringing and finally I picked it up.

CHAPTER 13

It was like going through the same nightmare twice in one night. Donovan said, "Shamus, I found another body."

"Good for you," I said.

"You better come over."

"Go to hell."

"Or I can send somebody for you."

He hung up. I knew he would not hesitate to send for me, so I put on my shoes, dashed cold water in my face and drove back out to the northwest side to the address he'd given me. As I drove, the address settled slowly into a groove in my mind and by the time I got there I was more or less prepared.

But not quite well enough. Because when I walked into the dreary cubicle of the run-down rooming house and saw the pulpy, hammered-to-death face of Howie Jones, Marta Sandor's erstwhile janitor, the only thing I could think of to say was, "Oh, no!"

Donovan was there, with two other cops, a sergeant I didn't recognize, and, sure enough, Robinson. I guess the photographer and lab men hadn't made it yet.

It was Robinson who took the offensive. I was leaning against the door I had just closed, trying not to look at poor Howie, and Robinson stepped forward briskly.

"This time, choir boy," he said, "we got you dead to rights. In this guy's pocket—" He was so enthusiastic that he had his hands on me before he could think it over. I shook him off and turned to Donovan.

"I tell you something, Lieutenant," I said, "if you don't call off this eager beaver, I will grind him to bits in front of your eyes. I'd just as soon start now."

"Oh yeah?" Robinson said, starting for me again.

"Robinson, lay off," Donovan snapped.

"But, Lieutenant—" I was staring at Robinson.

"Didn't he come up from the vice department?" I said.

Robinson glared at me.

"What's it to you?" he said.

I looked at Donovan again.

"He's really trying to make good," I said. "He went to see Ben Champlain all by himself. He wasn't even on duty."

Donovan moved slowly to look at Robinson.

"That's right now?" he said.

"I was trying to work something out," Robinson mumbled. "Had an idea—" Donovan's eyes were gray and steady on his face.

"You didn't tell me you went to Champlain's."

"No, Lieutenant. He didn't have nothin' to say, so I—"

"Then you wasted some of your own time?"

"I guess so, Lieutenant."

Donovan spoke quietly.

"All right. Now lay off the shamus, sit down and keep your mouth shut. It's a short trip back to the vice squad."

The fact that Donovan had called him down in front of me meant two things: that Donovan was under a great strain, and that I now had a long-term enemy in Robinson. I could only try to cut the thing short and get away. I pointed to the man on the floor, twisted and huddling, his arms still bent close to his head where he had thrown them trying to protect himself. I spoke to Donovan.

"This man was waiting in front of my office at one-thirty, when I got in my car to go to Ben Champlain's. He rode out there with me. On the way…"

I told him everything Howie had told me, as I remembered it. I told how I had let him out, after giving him twenty-five dollars, and how he had looked walking away.

"He showed me a picture of a girl on a white shag rug," I said. "But the head had been cut out and the print was in bad shape. I couldn't see anything familiar in it."

Donovan listened in silence. I got the door open.

"That is all I know about this man—or about how he came to die," I said. "You know where to find me."

I backed through the door, closed it quickly and went down the hall to the head of the stairs. I felt sick to my stomach and I grabbed the banister, closed my eyes hard and took half a dozen deep breaths before going on down to my car.

The thin, twisted body of Howard Jones went with me all the way.

"What the hell," he had said, "I got nothin' more to lose."

The "dirty little tramp" had turned into an angel.

Or was it the other way around?

* * * *

There was a phone message from Dottie Ellender and I called her at home. It took a long time to get an answer. When she came on, I said,

"Sorry to get you up."

"Up, hell!" she said. "I was in the shower. I wish you guys would work days."

"It ain't dark yet," I said. "What have you got?"

"Just a minute."

After a while she came back.

"That stuff you wanted—"

"Go ahead."

"Marta Sandor, Inc. A closed corporation. President and treasurer, Barney Sorelle; Vice-President, John Feldman; Secretary, Peter Chandler. Incorporated July, 1949; dissolved August, 1951. The business was in the black when they quit."

"Who are Feldman and Chandler?"

"You didn't ask for that, but I just happened to find out—Feldman is Sorelle's attorney. Chandler is an accountant."

"Thanks, Dottie," I said. "Send me a bill."

"Could I take it out in trade?"

"What do you need?"

"I need to collect some past due accounts."

"O. K. Send me a list of names."

"Good-bye, Mac."

I hung up and crawled into bed.

CHAPTER 14

I slept maybe two hours and when I woke I was groggy and my eyelids were sandpaper. I took a shower, shaved and put on a fresh shirt. By then it was seven-thirty in the evening, dark already and another fog had come in. I went across the street to Tony's and had a steak and several cups of coffee. The waitress got a little sassy and I barked at her and began to feel better. At eight-thirty I left, picked up the early morning edition of the *Tribune* and took it back to the office.

George had broken the story about Marta Sandor's so-called father, but he was cautious with it and didn't play it up. He used the Barney Sorelle tie-up as a lead and gave it a few paragraphs. It was an old familiar tale. Sorelle had denied any connection with the girl or her death, had stated that he didn't even know her and that he resented the newspaper's prying into his affairs.

He had probably stated plenty more, such as that any goddam private eye around town who might have opened his trap about Barney Sorelle was in for a fat surprise. But George had left that out.

From the Sorelle lead, the story went into the coroner's report on the cause of her death. George had put in the whole thing, technical language and all, to pad the piece out. He got to Peterson along toward the end and made quite a character of him, but without ridiculing him. You could tell by the way he'd written it, he was still feeling his way, hoping for a really big break. Apparently he hadn't got anything new from Donovan. He hadn't mentioned the name of Krupp, but had said that police were checking on a number of suspects. Which was probably a lot of crap.

I threw the paper away, and went outside again. It was after nine o'clock and Donovan had said he was pulling his man out of the dead girl's apartment at nine o'clock.

I started to get in the car, then changed my mind and left it parked. The walk might help stir up my mind. The fog wasn't so thick as it had been the night before, but the walks and streets were damp by the time I got to Chicago Avenue and made the short distance to Walton Place. There were no police cars parked in front of the place now and no reporters. The street was dark and empty, except for the tenants' cars along the curbs and one middle-aged lady who was walking a French poodle.

At the entrance to the building I scouted the line of cars, trying to check on whether Donovan's man had one waiting for him. I didn't see anything that looked like a city car, so I went on in. The foyer door was still open and I got in the elevator and went up to the eighth floor. I didn't meet anyone.

The apartment door was closed and no light showed under it. I listened with my ear against the panel and heard nothing. I tried the knob, but the door was locked. Donovan, or his man, had forgotten; or the official mind had been changed.

I found the key Norman had given me and let myself in, making sure the door was locked behind me. I stood for a minute in the dark beside the planter rail and tried to get a feeling for the place. The odor of perfume still lingered faintly in the room and brought back the memory of Marta Sandor as I had seen her the night before. That wasn't the feeling I wanted to have, so I snapped on a light.

Everything was in order. The white shag rug lay smooth and flat on the floor. There were three pillows lined up across the back of the davenport. They had print covers with large, floral designs. I didn't know how many sweating cops had leaned against them in the last few hours but I thought I might as well see what I could find.

I picked up one of the pillows and turned it over. There were large dark areas in the prints and it was hard to see anything. I sniffed it and got only the odor of cloth. There was a floor lamp at one end of the davenport and I turned that on. It had a strong bulb in it and gave a white light.

I sniffed each pillow in turn and held each under the strong light. I knew Donovan would have gone over them thoroughly and it wasn't likely that he had missed anything. Still, I had to do something.

The one in the middle gave off a trace of scent. I held it under the light and looked it over. The material was heavy and coarse, maybe a rayon, and so colorful that even if there had been something on it, or if it had been scratched, it wouldn't have shown much. Both Donovan and I had assumed that the method of killing had been with a pillow held over the face till the girl suffocated. This was because there were no marks of strangulation. According to this assumption, the pillow that had been used would have to show something—at least small tears made by the girl's teeth, even though, having been knocked out previously, she might not have put up much fight. Of course, it wouldn't have to be this pillow or any of these three. But Norman had said he'd found one of the davenport pillows lying near the body.

I looked around the room to rest my eyes. A narrow hallway led out of the living room to a bedroom and bath at the opposite end of the room from the door. I went into the hall and a gleaming chrome and porcelain

71

bath was visible through a partly open door. A door on my left led into a spacious dressing room, with a curtained arch between it and the bedroom. Both walls of the dressing room were lined with wardrobe space, wooden sections with sliding doors. I walked between them into the bedroom.

It was nearly as large as the living room, with an oversized double bed, covered with a blue satin spread, smooth and untouched. The pillows at the head had been rolled and showed as a single, neat cylinder across the headboard. I pulled back the satin spread and looked at them. They were unwrinkled and the slips were fresh and unused. They gave off the scent of a delicately perfumed laundry soap, but nothing more personal than that.

I felt silly sniffing everything in the place so I quit it and trusted my eyes. The furniture in the bedroom was modern, elegant and carefully matched. I opened the top drawer of a low chiffonier and found gloves, handkerchiefs and purses, all empty of papers or anything else that might have told a story.

The next two drawers contained lingerie—all types and colors. I pawed through the garments, trying not to disarrange them, looking for anything I could find—theater ticket stubs, pawn tickets, receipted bills. And I didn't find anything.

In the dressing room I pushed back the sliding doors over the wardrobe and went through the dresses, suits and coats hanging there. None of them had "Marta Sandor" labels and I found nothing in any of the pockets. Whatever else the girl may have been, she had certainly been neat. Also, she had an ample and well-rounded wardrobe, from the skin out. No doubt she had worn it beautifully.

I went back to the living room, stood there a minute, then remembered the highball glass which Norman said he had returned to the kitchen shelf. I crossed the room, passed through the dinette, then through a swinging door into the kitchen. It was all steel, all electric and like everything else in the apartment, all in order. The empty highball glass on the shelf under a high cupboard was the only item in the room that was out of place.

I stuck my nose over it, ducking down to avoid the cupboard, and smelled it. Apparently Norman had not only replaced it on the shelf, he had also rinsed it out. There was no odor. Out of habit, though it probably no longer mattered, I refrained from touching the glass itself. There were traces of lipstick around the rim.

No whisky bottle was in sight. I looked in the cupboards, but found no bottle.

Police lab, I thought. The bottle must be Donovan's blunt instrument.

It checked. A nearly full bottle would knock a person out. But if you hit hard enough to kill him, the bottle would probably break. So she must have been struck just hard enough to make her unconscious.

I switched off the kitchen light and returned to the living room. The three pillows sat there on the davenport. It seemed for a moment as if they were staring back at me. It also seemed, as often in the past, that Donovan had been right when he'd said I wouldn't find anything.

I found myself looking at the white shag rug. Pretty soon I was on my hands and knees, going over it inch by inch, exploring the loose nap with my fingers. It was like going through a miniature jungle, but it was the cleanest rug I had ever seen, notwithstanding all the activity on it in the last forty-eight hours. Apparently there was nothing to be found on it except an occasional grayish smudge where a policeman's foot had paused in passing.

I paid particular attention to the smudges. There were a dozen of them, grayed spots where the nap had been pushed down flat. I brushed these spots up, loosening the nap with my fingers. Suddenly I remembered Howie, "tidying up" after Miss Sandor. My fingers stiffened, then relaxed and I thought, but Howie is dead. Somebody has to carry on.

And then I thought, Easy, Mac!

I brushed my fingers lightly over the remaining smudged spot and started to get up. Then one finger brushed against a small, cold ridge and I stayed down long enough to roll up onto the palm of my hand a silver chain, very thin and delicate, about two inches long, with a sharp pin on one end and a paper-thin pendant on the other—an item such as a man might wear on his lapel to hold a boutonniere. The pendant, the size of a nickel, was engraved and I carried it to the lamp to study it. I made out the words, "Happy Birthday to Barney—from Marta." Below this was a date, but the engraving was so fine I couldn't read it.

I glanced at the small, blonde desk where, the night before, I had found my name marked in the telephone directory. Sometimes people have magnifying glasses.

I dropped the pin into my coat pocket and went to the desk. It had a wide center drawer above the kneehole and smaller drawers on each side. They were all locked. The lock was on the center drawer, a simple little lock that ought to yield to almost any instrument. I didn't see any scratches on it and wondered whether Donovan had opened it. I couldn't imagine his passing it up, but unless he had found a key, there would have been some marks to show that he'd forced it.

I got out a penknife and went to work on it, working carefully, trying not to mark the shiny, metal surface. The knife made faint scratching sounds. I couldn't find the point at which the tumbler would give. It was a tight, well-made lock. I began to lose patience, twisted the knife, almost breaking it, and held myself still for a minute till my hand steadied.

And then, over the sound of my breathing, over the distant purring of traffic in the streets below and an occasional wave of muted music from a radio somewhere in the building, there came another sound—the sound of a key in the lock of the apartment door, and I stood there, illuminated by the lights I had switched on myself, with my knife sticking in the lock of the desk, and froze, trying to think of the people who now had keys to the place.

I could think of only one. Barney Sorelle.

It was too late to hide and anyway, there was no place to do it. I jerked the knife out, dropped it into my pocket and straightened. I was wearing a gun and I unbuttoned my coat and turned to face the door. My right hand traveled toward the holster as the door swung open.

The foliage in the planter forming the vestibule screened whoever had entered, but apparently did not screen me. There was a moment of dead silence. Then the door closed and latched itself quietly and a woman's voice said, "Well—hello."

There was no fear in the voice and certainly no threat. I let my hand relax and stood waiting. She let me wait quite a while. Then she came slowly around the end of the planter.

A black purse dangled from her left hand and in the other she carried a pair of gloves. She came on into the room, moving gracefully and with economy, and she was a knockout. Small and blonde, with one of those sweet, innocent faces, and a body that must have been put together by hand in whatever workshop it is they come from—the Harlows, the Wilsons and the Monroes.

She walked to the davenport, dropped the gloves and purse onto it and stood there, waiting for me to say something. Her eyes went over me in that subtly appraising feminine way and then, as mine met them and held bravely, she dropped long lashes over them and smiled slowly, secretly. After a moment she opened them again, wide, looked directly into mine and said, "My name is Marta Sandor. What's yours?"

74

CHAPTER 15

There wasn't much to gain by playing guessing games with her. I told her my name. She thought it over briefly and said, "You're the private eye. I read about you sometimes. In the papers."

"Have you read the papers recently?"

"Not for a while. I don't read much. It strains my eyes."

She gave me that slow smile again.

"Been out of town?" I asked.

"I was in Hollywood."

"I should have guessed."

She had a good laugh. Low, free and on the sexy side.

"I wasn't making a picture," she said. "I was just visiting a friend."

"I imagine you have plenty of them."

"A girl can't have too many friends."

She seemed completely willing to let me lead the conversation. If it had been my place and I'd come home to find a stranger in it, I would have asked all the questions, hard and fast and doubtless in a loud voice.

"Was one of your friends a girl named Diana Peterson?"

"You mean Dinny? Oh sure."

I swallowed.

"Maybe you'd like to sit down," I said.

She sat down on the edge of the davenport and crossed her knees. She put one elbow on the top knee, rested her beautiful chin on the palm of her lovely little hand and gazed at me with her blue eyes.

"Were you awfully fond of her—of 'Dinny'?" I asked.

"We're good friends. She spends a lot of time here."

"Well, hold on tight, Marta…Dinny is—gone."

Her eyes widened. I wouldn't have thought it was possible.

"Gone?" she said.

"She's dead."

She lifted her head from her hand. A wave of pain traveled over her face. Then it cleared again and that heavenly smile broke through.

"Oh, no," she said simply. "Dinny wouldn't die. You've made a mistake."

"I'm afraid not. She died in this apartment, last night."

She looked around the room and her face was bewildered.

"But she wouldn't just—die," she said.

"She didn't just die," I said. I looked around the room myself, wishing Donovan would step out of the wall and take over. "May I sit down?"

She patted the seat of the davenport with her hand. I sat down, not too close. I began to tell her about it, easing across the rough places, trying to tell her only enough to make her understand. When I finished, her face had that hurt look again. I was sure it was the same kind of look she would have for anyone—or probably any animal—who had been hurt or killed.

After a while she said, "It was Norman who found her?"

"Yes."

She shook her head.

"Poor Norman. It must have been awful."

"You knew him?"

"I never met him."

"Did you know he used to come here to the apartment to see her?"

"No. But Dinny's been using the apartment for quite a while now. I haven't been here much lately."

"Then Dinny must have told Norman about you."

"I don't think so. She wanted him to think this was her apartment."

"I guess that's what he thought. She told him she was Marta Sandor."

"Yes."

I began to feel mixed up.

"You *are* Marta Sandor?"

"Oh yes."

"But you let Diana Peterson use your name and your apartment."

Her blue eyes widened, as if she were looking for a way to explain to me.

"You see—Dinny thought I was wonderful."

"You were. You are," I said.

Hold on, Mac, I thought. Hold on real tight.

"She wanted to be me really. She never got much of a break."

"Then she was just playing Norman Krupp for a sucker?"

She had her chin on her hand again and her blue eyes were frank and honest.

"He was in love with her," she said. "If he wanted to take her out—give her things—what's wrong with that?"

She had me.

"Nothing's wrong with it," I said. "Excuse me."

That misery was in her face again.

"Do you think she suffered very much?" she said. "Dying that way, I mean—"

"Not for long," I said. "It must have been very quick."

"Poor Dinny," she said. "She never had a break. She had a little room —just a room, with a hot plate." She shifted her position on the davenport and her head came around as she looked at me. It was as if she were trying to shake off the mood and find a new one. "So I would ask her to come here. She liked coming here. When I went away, naturally she stayed while I was gone."

"Why did you go away?" I asked.

She looked away then.

"I—wanted a change."

"That was why you closed down the dress business?"

She looked at me quickly.

"The dress business? Yes. We closed it down."

"What did Aaron Krupp think about that?"

"Aaron?" She seemed startled. Then she laughed that quick, soft laugh. "I didn't even ask him."

"Even though you knew him quite well?"

She had folded her legs under her on the davenport and now she ran a finger slowly along the edge of one shoe as she talked. It was a very small shoe.

"Mr. Krupp was very good to me," she said. "I would never have bothered him with such a problem."

After a moment she said, "Are you acquainted with Mr. Krupp?"

"Slightly."

"He's a wonderful man."

"That he is."

She got up suddenly, looked at me, leaning toward me a little, appealing.

"Could we get out of here—for a while?" she said. "I don't feel good in here now."

"Certainly." I stood up. "I don't have a car with me. Shall I order a cab?"

"That would be nice. I'll freshen up."

"You look fine," I said, meaning every word of it.

I got the good, slow smile again.

"You're sweet, Mac," she said.

No, I thought, I'm not very sweet. But sometimes I'd be willing to try.

She went into the hall toward the bathroom and I found the telephone on a shelf under the vestibule planter. I called the cab company and ordered one at the building address. Because cab drivers have a lot of time

77

to sit around and read the papers, I did not mention the apartment number. I said we would come down and if the driver had to wait a few minutes, then he could wait and we would pay the tariff. Then I hung up and waited for her to come back into the room.

That's all I did. I just waited. I didn't think about anything or try to figure anything out. I just sat and waited, wishing she would hurry up so I could see her again.

It wasn't long really, but it seemed long. I was turning my hat over and over with my hands when she came out of the hallway, wearing a different hat, carrying a different purse and another pair of gloves. Otherwise she looked the same as the first time I had seen her, which was a hell of a good way to look.

I stood up and we headed for the door. There were two handsome pieces of luggage just outside, which she must have had some attendant bring up for her, and she looked at them and hesitated. I picked them up and carried them into the apartment.

"Where did you want them?" I asked.

She just shook her head slowly, wrinkling her pretty brow.

"I just remembered," she said, "I haven't called Barney."

"Oh?"

"To tell him I'm home."

The skin was tight along my jaw.

"You have to call him?"

She looked at me with the wide eyes.

"I always call Barney."

"All right," I said. "I'll wait."

She gave me that appraising look again and her brow cleared and the wrinkles were transferred to her nose, where they looked a lot better.

"Barney can wait a while," she said.

I dropped the bags, closed the door firmly, and offered my arm. She took it and we walked down the corridor to the elevator.

My emotions were about as mixed as they ever get.

CHAPTER 16

In the cab she sat close to me and I settled back against the cushion and inhaled a little of the scent she wore. When I found that it failed to demolish me, I got up some nerve again.

"This Barney you mention," I said. "Would he be the gentleman about town who sometimes gets into the papers?"

"Barney Sorelle," she said quietly.

"I met him today for the first time."

There was some silence. Then she said, "Barney's all right. He's always been good to me."

I had disliked him from the beginning. Now I was hating him savagely. Unreasonably, but savagely and truly.

"How did you meet him?" she asked.

"He wanted me to go to work for him."

She gave me a quick look.

"And you didn't take the job?"

"I was busy on another case."

She looked out the window. We were on Michigan Avenue, moving slowly toward the Loop.

"Barney doesn't like to be turned down," she said.

"He didn't like it at all."

"What did you do?"

"I hit him."

She seemed a little startled. It was the first time she had shown that type of reaction and I wondered how deep her poise really went.

"Oh?" she said. "Just because you didn't want to work for him?"

"No. Because he snarled at me."

After a while she said, "Barney's impulsive. He's like a little boy."

"That's what I told him."

"Well, that's all right. I have to tell him that sometimes myself."

Pretty soon I said, "Well, we got through that one."

"What do you mean?"

"I mean I didn't know how you would take it when I told you I had hit Barney."

"How did I take it?"

79

"You took it fine."

"Good for me," she said.

"Good for you."

I couldn't tell about her. I couldn't tell whether she was as relaxed as she seemed to be or whether she held a tight rein on herself and underneath was a bundle of ragged nerves. Maybe I would find out eventually if I should have the good luck to know her that long. And maybe I would. I had been very lucky in my time.

I thought I ought to tell her about Howie Jones, but I couldn't bring myself to do it.

Not yet, I thought. Don't push the old luck. Let her get used to you gradually.

"This Diana Peterson," I said, "was she your roommate? Didn't she ever have a place of her own?"

"Just what I mentioned," she said. "A little room. Would you like to see it?"

"Maybe it's got a new tenant."

I didn't mean it the way it sounded. Marta was shocked.

"Already?"

"Sorry," I said. "I was thinking, if she's been using your apartment— maybe she gave the other place up."

"No. She kept some of her things there."

"If you'll tell me where it is—" She told me a number on Ontario Street and I gave it to the driver. He made a quick left turn and then moved slowly along Ontario to the Apollo Hotel. It was one of those faded, third-class hotels that are sprinkled all over town, with rates by day, week or month and facilities for "light housekeeping." I got out, paid the fare and asked the driver to wait. Marta took my hand and stepped out onto the sidewalk. Her hand was small and warm. She held my arm as we turned toward the building entrance and her fingers bit lightly into my flesh. The cab driver switched off the lights.

We started up the steps that led to the ornately framed glass doors of the building. There was a wide landing in front of the door, stretching on either side into deeply shadowed recesses. Beyond the door, dimly lighted, was the dingy, depressing foyer of the old hotel.

As my foot hit the top step, the door opened and two men came out. They seemed to be in a hurry and we stepped back to let them pass. Since I had eyes only for Marta Sandor, their faces rang no bell in me till they stopped suddenly, two steps down, and turned to look back at us. Then I saw who they were. One of them, the ex-pug, I was seeing for the third time; the other I had seen only once before, when the two of them had confronted me at Ben Champlain's studio.

At the moment, they were loaded down. Each of them carried a large carton—large and heavy. They were not at their best, standing there with hunched shoulders, holding the boxes, gawking at us.

Marta's fingers were tight on my arm, but her voice was calm and clear. She nodded to them, saying, "Hello, Bronk—Alex."

They nodded back in some confusion, mumbling, "Miss Marta..."

Their manner was extremely respectful. But they were clearly surprised to see her. They were so surprised that it didn't seem to matter that I was there too. They saw only the girl.

Marta turned to the door and the two lads were still gazing at her. I stood there, waiting, and after a moment, they turned away and went on toward the street. At the sidewalk they turned left toward the Lake.

"Excuse me a moment," I muttered and left Marta to return to our waiting cab. I leaned into the window to speak to the driver. "There'll be a car pulling out of here," I said, holding out a ten dollar bill. "Follow it, please. There are at least two guys in it and when they stop, they'll unload a couple of cartons."

Headlights flickered on down the street. The driver looked at me uncertainly.

"I'm no cop—" he started.

I groped for my wallet, jerked it out and opened it, exposing a photostat of my license. He leaned toward me to read it. There was the sound of a gunned motor and the headlights swung away from us, straightened and passed.

"All I want is to know where they go," I said.

I told him where my office was and that he could wait for me there. "I'll pay for waiting time," I said.

He had his motor going.

"Sure, Mac," he said.

I dropped the ten spot on the seat and pulled back as he got away from the curb. I stood a moment, watching him go, then turned again to the hotel, went up the wide steps and into the dimly lighted foyer. Marta was waiting, her face pressed against the glass.

"I should have called Barney," she said.

I waited, my skin crawling up the back of my neck. But pretty soon she slipped her arm snugly under mine and looked into my face.

"Mac, will you stay close to me tonight? I'm a little scared."

I felt big and strong, like Paul Bunyan or Davy Crockett.

CHAPTER 17

We walked up two flights of stairs on worn, frayed carpeting. The building was quiet, probably because it was early in the evening and the tenants were all out. Who would stay here if there was somewhere else to go? Marta walked close to me, holding my arm. Now and then her fingers would tighten and dig in.

She led me to a room on the third floor at the rear of the building. She tried the door, then searched through her purse till she found a key.

Dingy as the foyer had been, the room we entered was worse. No matter how I worked on it, I couldn't fit the beautiful girl on the white shag rug into this apartment. It was much the same as Peterson's on LaSalle Street, except that this one had a bath of its own.

Paint had chipped away from the old-fashioned chest of drawers in one corner. There was a studio couch with a drab brown cover that sagged in one corner. Padding showed through the raveled upholstery of an over-stuffed rocker. A dusty curtain covered the entrance to an alcove at one end and in the alcove were a hot plate, a small ice-box and some shelves. Another curtained alcove led through a narrow dressing room into the bath. The one window in the room looked directly out on the brick wall of the building next door, twenty feet away.

I looked around and I looked at Marta and I said, "I don't believe it."

"I wouldn't lie to you, Mac."

"I know it. But I can't make this fit with the girl we found in your apartment. She must have been very beautiful. I remember thinking that."

"She was a strange girl. She had a lot of problems."

I tried to read her face, but it held only her beauty and a little sadness.

"Was Carl Peterson one of her problems?" I asked.

She didn't answer right away.

"She tried to get away from him—but he had some hold over her. She was trying to get away from him when she began using my apartment."

I began to look the place over, opening dresser drawers and looking through them for whatever I could find. Marta sat on the studio couch and waited, watching me.

I didn't find much. The drawers contained a few skimpy, worn items of lingerie, some cheap blouses and a couple of skirts.

"Did she wear your clothes, too?" I asked.

"Sometimes," Marta said. "You see—she didn't have anything!"

"Clearly she didn't," I said. "So what I keep wondering is why would anybody go to the trouble of killing her?"

A shiver went over her.

"Please," she said.

"I'm sorry."

The bottom drawer of the dresser was empty, except for a couple of pamphlets—Carl Peterson type. They were both titled, *The End of the World—Are You Prepared?* The printing was mediocre and the paper was cheap and pockmarked. There were eight pages, saddle-stitched down the middle. I picked one up and sat on the floor to read it.

The first inside page was more of the same stuff Peterson had preached about when George Keeler and I had visited him earlier. Evil and devastation. On the inside of the cover was the imprint: Salvation Publishing Company, P. O. Box 1802, Chicago. The author of the pamphlet was Carl Peterson.

I had neither the time nor the inclination to read the stuff, but I turned the pages, stalling, while I tried to think what to do next. And in turning the pages, I learned the pamphlet was illustrated.

Beginning on Page 4, under the chapter heading: "The Wages of Sin," there was a halftone picture of a man and woman, half seated, half reclining, on a davenport. Apparently they had just emerged from an embrace. This illustration, according to the caption, pointed up the evils of necking. It wasn't a very good reproduction job, but certain things about it were clear enough.

The woman in the scene was unquestionably the dead brunette, Diana Peterson. It took a moment longer to identify the man as the pug whom Barney Sorelle had brought along on his visit to my office. Marta had called him "Bronk." But most interesting was the davenport on which they sat, especially the pattern of the pillow covers, which I had gone to some trouble to examine.

I handed it up to Marta, who sat, still watching me, on the studio couch.

"It was taken in your apartment," I said.

"Yes," she said.

"Did you know that was going on?"

"I don't see anything so bad about it," she said. "Except it isn't a very good picture of Dinny."

"Do you know the man in it?"

"We saw him tonight. His name is Bronk. He works for Barney."

I reached for the book again, but she held it, even drew it back a little.

83

"What are you looking for?" she asked.

"If there was one, there may be more," I said.

"Can't you just forget it, Mac?"

"I don't see how. Nothing can hurt her anymore."

"But there are others."

She had let go of the book and I was busy looking at it. I didn't answer. I felt her breath then, close and warm on my neck and she said, "There's me."

I stopped looking at the book.

Indeed there is, I thought.

I looked up at her, took one of her hands.

"I guess I haven't told you everything," I said.

"Everything about what?"

I told her about being called to her apartment by Donovan and my name being marked in the phone book. I told her about running into Norman Krupp later.

"The girl was frightened about something," I said. "Maybe she thought of calling me. Then Barney Sorelle showed up with his pitch. Then there's Norman Krupp, who is a bright, promising boy."

She looked at me steadily and I couldn't guess what she was thinking.

"I didn't want to get into it," I said. "I keep busy. I don't like murder and death and I never get enough sleep. But I'm into it now, for three reasons: one is Donovan, two is Norman Krupp and the third is the dead girl. I think maybe now there's a fourth reason."

Her blue eyes were wide and questioning.

"What is the fourth one, Mac?"

"A girl named Marta Sandor."

Her eyes remained, wide and steady, on mine.

"Do the police think Norman Krupp killed her?" she asked.

"I don't know," I said. "Maybe. I'm trying to figure things out."

After a moment her eyes shifted, then looked down. I was watching her and I saw fear creep slowly into her face. Her hand went to her throat as she stared downward. I followed the direction of her gaze.

A couple of pages of the pamphlet had flipped over while we talked and there was a new illustration. It showed another couple on the same davenport. The gown the girl was wearing was much more décolleté than in the first picture. The amorous attitude was more exaggerated and except for a slightly stiff look about the girl's head, much more realistic. The man in the picture was younger than Sorelle's gorilla, dressed in a dark suit and his face was truly, genuinely adoring of the girl. All in all, it was a lot better picture; but also, it was a lot more shocking than the other.

Because the young man in it was Norman Krupp and the girl was Marta Sandor.

CHAPTER 18

She lifted the book by one corner, holding it away from her as if it had been a piece of soiled linen. Finally she tore her eyes from it and looked at me.

"Mac," she said softly, "it's me."

"I noticed."

She shook her head.

"But I never did that."

I looked into her beautiful blue eyes and I believed it; partly because of her tone, partly because I couldn't help myself. I wanted to believe it.

She looked at the photo again.

"Who is that man?" she said.

"You don't know?"

"I never saw him before this."

"Truly?"

She looked at me.

"It's Norman Krupp," I said.

The pamphlet slipped out of her hand and I picked it up and studied the new picture. There was something wrong about it but it took a while to find it. When I did, it seemed too obvious. The wrongness lay in the stiff set of the girl's head. It was Marta's head all right, but it was on the wrong body. This was clear enough in the extra thickness of the neck, where the faking head ended, and in the way the head was turned unnaturally on the shoulders.

I turned back to the first illustration and compared the girls' figures from the neck down. It was inconclusive because of the different cut of the dresses, until I saw the distinctive mark in the hollow of the throat. It was the same in both pictures, a small mole, barely visible, but there, un-mistakably, in exactly the same place as I had seen it on the dead girl her-self.

So the head of Marta Sandor had been pasted over the head of Diana Peterson on another print and then rephotographed to produce the faked picture.

I explained it to Marta. She listened abstractedly. Her hands were tight fists on her knees, and when I touched one of them in was cold as ice.

"I don't understand," she said, not to me but into the air, "why she would do these things to me! I tried to help her——"

I decided maybe she needed a few minutes of privacy and turned my head away to glance through the rest of the pamphlet. After a while I looked up at her. She was still in that tense position on the couch and it was very quiet in the room.

"Maybe you'd better tell me about it," I said. "Because there's another picture in the book, honey. And it's of you too."

It was a picture I'd seen before—a nude girl lying on a white shag rug, and the caption underneath read:

"The Wages of Sin. This Girl Is Dead."

On the inside of the back cover, facing the picture, was a brief statement that said, "Send for more booklets on *The Wages of Sin*... P.O. Box 1802," etc.

If this one ends with a nude on a white rug, I thought, I wonder what the next series is like? This could be the greatest come-on since the earliest purveyors of snake-oil.

The halftone was not good enough to show the mole on the neck, if there was a mole, and I had no way of telling whose body it was, even though I'd seen Diana's at close range. But the face and the hair were Marta Sandor's. I handed the booklet up to her.

She looked at it dully, without expression, the way you keep looking at a scene of horror long after your shock reaction has worn off, when you register no more horror, but only a kind of numbed fascination.

To give her a little more time, I went over the rest of the apartment, I did it completely, without missing anything and without much regard for what got disarranged in the room. I found no more pamphlets, no more pictures—at first—nothing of any interest at all, until I looked into the dressing room alcove near the bathroom. There I found a suitcase.

It caught my eye because it was new. A cheap make, but new and shiny. There was a bus company baggage tag on it and that looked new too. I lifted the bag and found it heavy enough to have contents. I laid it flat on the floor, opened it quietly and went through it.

It contained ladies' apparel, a good supply of it, and unlike the things I had found in Diana Peterson's dresser, these were new and fresh. Like the suitcase, they were low-priced, but they weren't old and worn out.

At first I thought it must be an emergency cache. If she had to go somewhere in a hurry, she'd want a bag packed and ready. I looked at the luggage tag to see where she might have been lately, but there was only a number on it.

I dug deeper into the bag and found a large, stiff, rectangular package wrapped in tissue paper. I lifted it out, unwrapped the tissue and found a small stack of photographs, glossy eight by ten prints. Some were mounted on large mats. There were several head shots, half a dozen full length. All but two of the head shots were fashion photos. They were what a model would carry as samples. They all showed the same girl, a pretty brunette of nineteen or twenty—not Diana Peterson. I knew she was not Diana Peterson, but I knew I had seen her somewhere. Somewhere not long ago.

I studied the pictures for a while, trying to remember, then I rewrapped them, replaced them in the suitcase, closed it and set it back where I had found it.

When I went back into the main room, Marta was sitting on the edge of the couch, her fists clenched on her knees. The booklet had fallen from her hand and lay on the floor at her feet. She didn't look at me when she spoke.

"I can't tell you much about it," she said, "because I don't know very much. But I knew she had done something with pictures—"

"Like the ones in the book here?"

"Not quite. I never saw these—"

"There were others?"

"Yes. Of Aaron Krupp."

"Aaron Krupp and you?"

Her eyes and her voice faltered.

"Yes—but not like these, Mac. Not in a book, printed, to send to thousands of people! I never dreamed she would do anything like this!"

She put her face in her hands and I was afraid she might break down. I couldn't let that happen. Not now.

"Listen," I said. "Until I have some reason to think another way, Aaron Krupp is a fine gentleman, and you are a great lady. Nothing you tell me now will change that opinion."

When she said nothing I moved closer to her.

"I have to know," I said. "Were there some pictures of you and Aaron Krupp?"

"Not like these!"

"All right. Like what?"

"There were pictures that had been taken at garment shows—for publicity. Mr. Krupp and I were in some of them."

"And Diana Peterson had these pictures?"

"Yes."

"Had they been—doctored? Faked up, like these in the book?"

"Not when I saw them. But she said they could be."

"What did she plan to do with them?"

88

"I don't know. I couldn't believe it—" I went to the studio couch and sat down beside her. I took one of her cold hands and held it tightly. It trembled in mine.

"Try to relax, honey," I said. "What about the pictures? How did you find out?"

"I was in Hollywood and this letter came—from her, from Dinny. She said she had changed her name, legally, to Marta Sandor. My name. She said she considered my apartment to be her own. She said it would be best for me to change my name too—to take hers."

"What advantage would there be for her in switching names?"

Marta looked at me.

"Skip that," I said. "I guess, little by little, it's becoming obvious. Even to me."

"It's just that she wanted it that way, Mac. She was—very strange."

"How long had you known her?"

"I don't know—two years maybe."

"And you liked her?"

"At first. She was just a young kid from some town nobody ever heard of."

"And she changed?"

There was quite a long pause.

"Yes. She changed."

"Who brought you together?"

"Barney. He was—interested in her. She began to model for the dress company, wearing our new numbers."

"Who did your photography?"

"A man named Ben Champlain. He had a studio right next door."

"And Barney brought you to her and said she was to be one of your models?"

"Yes. He wanted me to help her along, teach her things."

"What kind of things?"

"How to dress—how to behave—how to—you know. The things a girl ought to know. In the city."

"And she was a good pupil?"

"Too good."

"What do you mean?"

She looked away.

"Nothing," she said. "I don't know how to explain it. She began to want to be me really—not just like me—but to take me over."

"And that was all right with Barney?"

"I think Barney was in love with her."

I got up and took a turn about the room. Her hands had relaxed now, but she still had that crushed, hopeless look.

"And after you got this letter," I said, "you came back and saw her and she put it up to you—either you would let her take over now, or she would make trouble tor Aaron Krupp?"

She nodded stiffly.

"Something like that."

"May I ask you one more direct question?" I said.

She looked up, her eyes held mine for a moment, then dropped away.

"Yes, Mac."

And I stood there and looked at her and finally I asked her the question that I didn't really want to ask, the question that I couldn't see had anything to do with the death of Diana Peterson, the question I had to ask, because now I had to know the answer, for myself, for my own peace of mind and nothing else.

"What does Barney Sorelle mean to you?"

There was a long silence. Then she said, "Barney Sorelle is my brother."

Outside in the hall there were quick footsteps, a key in the door. I had time to turn my head before it opened and a girl came in. A brunette. The one whose pictures I had found in the suitcase. The girl I'd seen on the stairs, asking the way to Carl Peterson's room.

CHAPTER 19

She stood there with one hand on the knob of the suddenly wide-open door, staring at us with a variety of expressions—from startled fear through confusion to exasperation and anger. Finally she stepped back and looked at the apartment number to make sure she hadn't opened the wrong door. Then she came on in slowly, pushing the door to behind her with her foot.

The dim light on Peterson's stairway and the photos I'd found in the suitcase had not done her justice. She was an extremely pretty girl, slim and well made, with dark eyes and truly black hair. Her face was slightly flushed now from shock and anger and there was quite a lot of light coming out of her eyes. When she found her voice it was full and confident and most of the shock had gone out of it.

"All right," she said, "who are you and what are you doing here?"

"This is your apartment?" I said.

"It certainly is."

"We didn't know it," I said.

"How did you get in?"

"We had a key. We were acquainted with the—former tenant."

"The former tenant might have told you—"

"The former tenant is dead."

That stopped her for a while. Her eyes traveled briefly over Marta, rigid again now on the studio couch, then looked at me curiously.

"I've seen you somewhere—" she said.

"Yes," I said. "On the stairway leading to Carl Peterson's apartment."

Fear slid back in her behind the eyes.

"You're from the police."

"No."

Having a momentary advantage, I decided to hold onto it by keeping my mouth shut. It worked all right. She wasn't hysterical, but she was scared enough to think things over and to want to know what was going on.

Pretty soon she was looking at the *End of the World* pamphlet that lay on the floor near Marta's feet. I let her wonder about that too. I don't know how much wondering she had to do but after a while she pulled her eyes away from it and looked at me again. She ran her tongue lightly over her lips.

"If you're not with the police—" she said, "then what—?"

"There will be police here sooner or later," I said. "This former tenant I spoke of did not die a natural death. She was murdered."

Except for a slight widening of her eyes, she took it pretty well. I wondered whether she had already known it.

Marta had stronger reactions. The springs of the sagging couch groaned and she was on her feet.

"Mac!" she said, and her voice was taut and strident. "Please get me out of here! I can't stand it."

This was not the Marta Sandor I had come to know and it scared me. I went to where she stood and put an arm around her. She was trembling now. The two women were staring at each other and Marta spoke first, the words coming in wrenched spurts.

"She looks like Dinny! She makes me think of Dinny!"

Now I understood that she trembled because she was crying and also fighting against crying.

"All right, baby," I said, "we'll go now."

The other girl's face was tense now too, but more puzzled than scared.

"Who's Dinny?" she said.

I didn't have time for her. I stooped, picked up the Peterson pamphlet from the floor and took Marta's hand. Then again there were footsteps outside, heavy ones this time and I waited for them to pass. But they stopped. I jerked my head at the brunette.

"Get away from the door," I said.

She moved to one side. The door opened and I stepped ahead to stand between it and Marta. There was a gun in my hand, but I put it away when I saw who was coming in. Robinson's unpleasant voice sneered in greeting.

"Well, the Boy Scout!"

I was happy to see him alone. But I wondered how he'd thought to come. Somebody would have had to tell him.

"Hello, Robinson," I said, "we were just leaving."

He was trying to look past me at Marta and I moved to block his view. He gave up trying and eyed the little brunette, who was standing off to my left, real scared now. Finally he looked at the booklet in my hand.

"I'll take that," he said, reaching for it.

"No," I said.

He scowled. It didn't help his face.

"The Lieutenant ain't got such a crush on you any more," he said. "You don't keep in touch."

"I'm not paid to keep in touch. When the Lieutenant comes around, he can have this."

I knew the conversation couldn't remain long on this formal level and I wanted to get out with Marta before Robinson started something foolish.

"Let's go now, honey," I said and heard her move close to me.

"I'd like to talk to the chick," Robinson said. "Both chicks."

"Later," I said.

I started to lead Marta past Robinson to the door and he put a hand on her arm, holding her.

"We'll wait for the Lieutenant," he said.

"Get your hand off her," I said. "The Lieutenant knows where to find me."

He didn't take his hand off. He just looked at me insolently. You have to take a certain amount of insolence in my business, but not from anybody like Robinson—or Barney Sorelle.

I let go of Marta's hand and put the pamphlet in it. She held onto it. Robinson was still holding her other arm and I chopped down hard on his wrist, driving his hand away. He started to swing at me and I stepped in close and hit him in the stomach. When he doubled over and charged me, head down, I took my time and put one where I wanted it on the back of his neck. He went down cursing, but started up again and I had to chop him down twice to make him stay on the floor.

I'd strained my wrist, handling him, and because of the inconvenient pain, I spoke a little abruptly to Marta.

"Let's go," I said, heading for the door.

When I didn't hear her footsteps behind me, I stopped and looked back. She was staring down at Robinson.

"I'm sorry I barked," I said. "There'll be more of them in a few minutes."

She kept on looking at Robinson.

"Is he with the police?"

"Currently, yes," I said.

I was looking at him now myself, waiting for him to come around and give me some trouble. The longer I looked, the harder I thought and suddenly I found myself on my knees beside him, going through his pockets. I worked carefully because I knew he wasn't completely unconscious and if he should come around, with me in that kneeling position, he could do a lot of damage.

There was a wallet in his coat pocket and I opened it. It was fat and bulky. I looked in where the bills should be and saw a couple of fives and some singles. They couldn't account for all the bulk. I probed deeper, found a wad of bills, folded over and clipped with an ordinary paper clip. They were all twenties and there were fifty of them.

A thousand bucks.

So it proved nothing. But it was a big wad to travel in the wallet of a civil service cop.

I replaced the bills and put the wallet back in his pocket, then straightened up and looked at Marta. When I held out my hand, she came to me, unsteadily walking around Robinson with her head in the air to join me at the door. We started out and the other girl said, "Wait! Please—"

I stopped and swung back. Marta kept going, her back to us, moving slowly with one hand on the wall, as if feeling her way.

"Well?" I said to the brunette.

"You can't leave me here alone—" I couldn't hang around arguing and I thought I might want to talk to her later.

"Then come along," I said. "Our time has run out."

I went ahead to catch up with Marta and the other girl, after hesitating for a moment, followed. She kept coming as I took Marta's arm at the head of the stairs and led her down into the dingy foyer. Outside, a squad car siren crooned a low, nervous sound.

"Is there a way out the back?" I asked the brunette.

She shook her head helplessly.

"This way," Marta said, turning back past the staircase toward the rear of the building.

There was a closed door, but she pushed it open and we were in a long narrow corridor with a red EXIT sign over a door at the far end. I passed Marta and held the door open. She stepped outside into a service area and the brunette followed her. We stood there for a minute among the garbage cans and then I found a door in the back fence that opened onto an areaway between the hotel and the next building. The areaway was open and clear through the block and we went into it, walked to the next street and turned over to Michigan, where I began looking for a cab. Marta walked close to me, but without touching me and the brunette came along beside Marta at some distance. It was around eleven o'clock now and there weren't many pedestrians on the sidewalks.

I looked past Marta to the other girl and said, "Would it be all right to ask your name—in case sometime we get into a conversation?"

She looked at me quickly, then looked away.

"My name is Sharon."

"Not Sharon 'Peterson' by any chance?"

This time she didn't look at me.

"Just Sharon," she said. "Who are you?"

"Call me Mac," I said. "May I present Miss Marta Sandor?"

Four strides later I realized that Sharon was no longer with us. I glanced over at where she had been, then looked back. She was standing, all alone in the middle of the sidewalk, stiff and straight, staring straight ahead.

I put my hand on Marta's arm and we both stopped. But Marta didn't look back. Instead, she turned to me slowly, her beautiful face twisted, her hands raised and clenched and suddenly she was leaning against me with her head on my chest and her tight fists beating a steady tattoo on my shoulders.

"Mac," she said, her voice muffled and distant, "Mac—what's happening? Why?"

"If I knew—" I said.

I didn't know how to handle this. I held her for a while and she quit pounding her fists. But we were on a public street, in front of the whole wide world—I wasn't sure it was legal. Anyway, I didn't want to have to explain anything to any prowling cops.

Beyond Marta's shoulder I saw that Sharon was in motion again, coming toward us. She came to within five or six feet and stopped. I gazed at her.

"What happened to you?" I asked.

She didn't answer. I held Marta, shifting her body so that I had one arm around her waist and if anybody noticed, it would look less like necking in public than as if I were only supporting her—as if, maybe, she were drunk. That would be easier to explain.

"Look, kids," I said, "let's not fall apart. Maybe we all ought to have a drink."

Through my head, like the refrain of a jazz tune, ran the question, Why is she falling apart?

I didn't know the answer to that, but I did know that if I couldn't handle one girl in the middle of the sidewalk on Michigan Boulevard, I sure as hell couldn't handle two of them.

A few doors north on our side of the street was a small cocktail lounge and I steered Marta that way. Sharon came along. By the time we reached it, Marta had pulled herself together enough to walk into the place under her own power. We found a booth in a corner and settled down. It was a circular booth and I sat in the middle, against the wall, between the two girls. It was dark and quiet in there, with few other customers. We ordered highballs all around and drank them slowly and in silence. Once Sharon said, "I'm sorry—I seem to be spoiling the party."

She made no move to leave. The girls were obviously, maybe deliberately, ignoring each other. But they spent a lot of time looking at me.

Old Uncle Mac, I thought.

Then I thought, We could just stay in here and drink. But eventually the place will close. I wonder whether there are any all-night joints where I could take two apparently respectable girls?

Marta was twisting herself this way and that and I saw she was examining her stockings. When she noticed me watching her, she smiled shyly.

"I snagged them on that couch," she said.

"I'll get you some new ones," I said, glad for a break, getting to my feet.

She put a hand on my arm.

"No, please—"

"Only take a minute," I said. "There's a drugstore across the street. What's the size and color?"

She gave me the specifications and moved so that I could slide past her out of the booth. I signaled the waitress and ordered another round of drinks.

"Be right back," I said.

I looked at Sharon.

"You need anything from the drugstore?"

She shook her head.

I left the place and jaywalked across Michigan to the drugstore. The girl at the hosiery counter was known to me. I had been in and out of that store many times, though never for this purpose. She found the hose for me, put them in a small paper sack and took my money without comment. As I turned away she said, "I never thought I'd see the day."

There is a snappy answer to that, but I was too preoccupied to make it. I just grinned at her. I guess it was a foolish kind of grin, because she started to laugh. I went out fast, bumping into three customers on the way. The third one turned out to be Aaron Krupp.

CHAPTER 20

We looked at each other, the way you do when you bump into someone you know and it takes a moment to realize it. I stood there with the sack full of nylons and he stood there, impeccable, with a paper neatly folded under one arm, and he had the advantage.

"Hello, Mr. Krupp," I said.

"Mac," he said, "I came now from your office."

"I'm sorry I wasn't in."

He gestured toward the soda fountain.

"This might do," he said.

I looked at him, at my package, and out the door.

"The boy," he said then. "He didn't come home from school yet."

My hand tightened on the package.

"The police came," he said.

"Donovan?"

"Donovan and some others."

My mind was moving in jerks, trying to get in high gear. I followed him to the soda fountain, where he ordered two lemonades.

He didn't waste any time but went right into his subject.

"Usually he comes home from the lab at five-thirty," he said. "Some days he works late, naturally. Today I said to myself, he shouldn't work so hard right now when he's upset. I took the car and went to the lab. Dark. All closed up. Likewise with the library. That is, not dark like the lab, but Norman wasn't there."

"Maybe he went somewhere with friends—for dinner."

"Not without calling Mama."

"But he's not himself now."

"He's a boy that remembers. Automatically, he would call."

"What did Donovan say?"

He shook his head ponderously.

"Nothing. Donovan sat and waited."

"For how long?"

"From four o'clock to after dinner."

"Then he'll be looking for Norman around town. All the cops will be looking for him."

His eyes were on me and I forced myself to meet them.

"And you, Mac?"

"Yeah," I said, "me, too. I'll be looking for him."

"It's a big town, Mac."

"I'll hire help," I said, getting down from the fountain stool.

He looked at me steadily for about half a minute. Then he reached into a pocket and pulled out a wallet. He took some bills out of it and handed them to me.

"If you hire help," he said, "you should have some more money."

"I'll keep an account of it," I said.

He brushed the thought aside.

"I trust you," he said. "It's only—the boy is close to the heart."

"Will you do this for me?" I said. "When you get home, go to Norman's room and go through his things; his clothes, desk, bureau—everything. Pick up all the match covers, ticket stubs, receipted bills, cards—all you can find."

"I never went through his things. I don't like to do it."

"I understand," I said. "But if you don't, then I'll have to and we can save time if you'll do it. I'll call you later for any names or addresses you find."

"If you say so, Mac."

"Try not to worry," I said.

I was good and worried myself. As Mr. Krupp had said, it was a big town. Also I had the ends of a lot of loose threads in my hand and I wanted the keep them separated till I was sure of the right way to tie them together. In order to do this, I would need more time than it appeared would be available.

Mr. Krupp waited while I went into a phone booth. I knew this guy, Larry Evans. He operated the same way I do, but he hadn't had all the breaks I'd had, and I could nearly always get him to work for me when he didn't have something else to do. He was dependable and hard working and he knew when to talk and when to keep still. I hoped, as I dialed the phone, that he would be in.

He was in, but he had gone to bed. His voice was gruff and tired when we started talking, but he came to life as we went along and I set it up for him to meet me at a Loop cafe, not far from the Randolph Street entrance to the I. C station. It would save time for him on this job to use a cab. He wouldn't have to worry about the parking problem and, riding in the back seat, he would have a chance to think about what he was doing. He promised to meet me in forty-five minutes.

Mr. Krupp walked outside with me.

"I picked up a taxi in front of your office, Mac," he said. "I think he was waiting for you."

We walked over to the cab. It was the driver I had sent to follow Sorelle's pugs from Ontario Street. He leaned toward the window, started to speak to me, then glanced at Krupp and closed his mouth.

"It's all right," I said. "Go ahead."

He still hesitated.

"This gentleman said he was waiting for you too—"

"Yeah. It's all right."

"First," he said, "they went to a joint on the West Side—the House of Jazz."

"Did they unload the boxes?"

"No. They split up. One guy drove off with the boxes, the other one took another car. I followed the one with the boxes. He took 'em to some photographer's place—Ben Champlain, the name was."

"All right, thanks," I said. "How much do I owe you?"

"Nothin'," he said. "The sawbuck covered it."

"Thanks again. I guess Mr. Krupp would like a ride home."

"O. K., Mac," the driver said.

Krupp got into the cab and I closed the door. The driver started the motor and I leaned into the open back window.

"Marta Sandor is back in town," I said.

Krupp blinked his eyes slowly.

"You've talked to her?"

"Yeah, some. Did you know she was Barney Sorelle's sister?"

He moved forward to sit on the edge of the seat, his elbows on his thighs, holding the neatly folded newspaper across his knees. His big face looked at me seriously through the window.

"I knew it, Mac."

"Did you ever figure that Sorelle might have furnished the capital to set her up in the dress business?"

"I thought of it. I never knew for sure."

"She never told you why she decided to go out of business?"

Mr. Krupp gave one of his massive shrugs.

"Did she ever talk to you about her brother?"

"Barney Sorelle?" He seemed to think it over. "Mac—is Sorelle involved in this case—this murder of the Peterson girl?"

"He sure is."

"Marta Sandor is a lovely girl, a truly fine individual."

"I am with you all the way."

"It wasn't her fault she had a brother like Barney Sorelle. As kids—she told me a little about it—they had a rough life. The kind I had as a kid, in

99

New York. Slums, poverty, dead end—"

"Yeah. I was there too."

"Then you know. The brother was older. I never met this Barney Sorelle, but I hear about him. Marta says he was always good to her, good big brother. Sent her to school. But when she says how good he was, she says it—too hard. I think maybe she was an investment to him."

"Uh-huh. But if the dress company was a good investment, why would he close it down?"

He shrugged again, looked away. I knew he was anxious to get on with the business of finding Norman and I felt for him.

"One thing more," I said, "have you been blackmailed recently?"

He was startled and looked at me wide-eyed.

"No," he said. "In fact, never."

I moved back from the cab window.

"O. K," I said. "But I think you would have been if the Peterson girl had lived."

He was still staring at me as the cab pulled away. I had forgotten about the nylons and the small paper sack fell out of my hand while I stood there. I stooped and picked it up and walked catty-cornered across Michigan to the cocktail lounge.

CHAPTER 21

Marta and Sharon were sitting across from each other in the booth, as I had left them. I didn't know whether they'd had any conversation during my absence, but they were not having any when I returned.

Marta's drink was only half gone. Her small hands were clenched again on the edge of the table and when she got up she turned to me, leaned heavily against me and let out a long sigh.

"You were gone so long!" she said.

"I ran into an old friend," I said.

She accepted the paper sack and excused herself to find a place where she could change. I sat down in the booth and ordered another drink.

Sharon was either too scared or too confused to say anything and I studied her for a minute. She had barely tasted her drink.

"How long have you known Peterson?" I asked.

She turned her head slowly and looked at me as if her mind had been a million miles away and had just walked back. Then she said, "Since this afternoon."

"And you never knew him before? From wherever you came from?"

"No."

"Where did you hear about him?"

Her eyes fell. When she looked up again some of her spirit had returned.

"Why do you ask so many questions?" she said. "It seems to me—"

"Yeah, I know. You're the one who ought to be asking questions. Look, I am a private detective…"

I told her who I was. I told her that a girl calling herself Diana Peterson had been killed, that this girl had modeled around town, that some of the modeling was for Peterson's religious pamphlets, but that some of it had been of a different nature. Finally I told her that Peterson had claimed the girl was his daughter, but that there was some strong doubt of this. Therefore, I was now asking her, Sharon, whether she had any previous connection with Peterson. She did not have to answer the question, but after all I was at work, on a touchy and urgent matter, that she had invited herself to the party and as long as she was with us, she might try to be helpful. She could hardly lose, unless she didn't trust me, which was all right with me, but in that case she would be better off to look up somebody else.

She took a sip of her drink and thought things over. She waited so long that I had given up expecting her to speak and was a little startled when she said, "I heard about Peterson at a place called the House of. Jazz. A night club. There's a girl working there who came from my home town. I went to see her."

"What does your friend do there?"

"She's a photographer. You know—those night club pictures—"

"I know. Why did you look her up?"

She hesitated.

"I was broke—didn't know where to go. She said maybe Mr. Peterson could give me a job."

"When was this—that you saw your friend? What was her name?"

"Dolly. Dolly Short." She was talking freely now, as if it were a relief to be able to talk. "She said she had an idea that Mr. Peterson could find a cheap room for me too."

"When was this?"

"Early this morning—real early—about four o'clock. The club doesn't close till maybe five or six."

"And this friend—Dolly—she mentioned only Peterson? No other names?"

"No. Just Peterson. She said Mr. Peterson was kind of eccentric, but he was all right. She said he was the fatherly type."

"What did you think when you met him?"

"I didn't like him. He was—very strange. Just sat and stared at me— and he talked like a fanatic. I though at first Dolly was playing a trick on me."

"He do anything out of the way? Make any passes?"

"No, nothing like that. He said he would have some work for me in a few days and in the meantime, he knew of a place I could live. He gave me some money in advance—twenty dollars."

"Did he say what the work would be?"

"He told me he was a publisher and that I would pose for illustrations for a new book."

"Didn't you wonder whether it was the kind of posing you would want to do?"

"I wondered—yes. But he didn't ask me to do anything right then, and I needed the money."

I looked at her.

"You're a good-looking girl. How could you be without a job?"

She laughed hollowly.

"Am I the only good-looking girl in Chicago? How many jobs do you think there are?"

I glanced around the place. Marta had been gone for quite a while. I decided to wait five more minutes and then ask Sharon to go check up.

"When he told you about the room," I said, "did he explain how he happened to know of it?"

"He said it had been rented by another girl who had worked for him, but she'd gone away."

"Gone away?"

"That bothered me a little. I asked him, 'What if she comes back?' and he said, 'She won't be back.'"

"Didn't you ask him any more questions about it?"

"Yes. I asked whether there was anything wrong about the room, and he said no. He said that if anything came up—if anybody asked me any questions, I could tell them he was my father and he would take care of everything."

"And even after that, you went ahead and moved in?"

"I had to have a room! I needed the money!"

"All right. One more question. Out there on the street, before we came in here, what made you so paralyzed when I introduced Marta Sandor?"

She looked away again and this time she hesitated. But when she answered she looked me straight in the eye.

"It was like—seeing a ghost. I heard about her at the House of Jazz. I overheard some girls talking. 'Marta Sandor is dead,' they were saying. I remembered the name. So when you said this girl was Marta Sandor, it threw me."

"That's all you heard them say? That Marta Sandor was dead?"

"Yes—except that most of them seemed to be happy about it."

I looked beyond her, past her shoulder, and said, "It's real nice of you to talk to me," I said, "but we won't talk any more now because I see Miss Sandor is coming back and she's a little upset."

"I'll say she is," Sharon said. "While you were gone, she did nothing but talk to herself."

"What about?" I asked quickly.

"I don't know—mostly she said, 'I ought to call Mr. Krupp. I ought to call—'"

"O. K., forget it," I said.

Marta came to the table then and she had regained a lot of composure. She was lovely, as she had been a couple of hours before in her own apartment, and on the surface anyway, she was relaxed. She gave me that good, frank smile. I stood up.

"I've got some work to do, baby," I said. "Can I take you home?"

She was a little startled.

"But it's so late, Mac!"

"I don't have regular hours."

After a moment, she tucked her arm under mine.

"All right," she said. "But do I have to go back to that apartment? I couldn't sleep there—"

"You don't have to go there. How about the Palmer House?"

"Whatever you say."

Sharon was climbing out of the booth and I didn't know what to do about her. I had invited her in and I couldn't walk away from her. But I wished she would wander away now. Still, wishing couldn't make it so. I guessed she had decided to hang around as long as possible and after that —what the hell? I didn't have time to ponder it. In another half hour I would have to meet Larry Evans. And we would have to look for Norman Krupp.

I nodded to Sharon and she followed us outside to the curb, where I flagged down a cab.

It was closing time for the theaters and traffic was heavy going north out of town. But toward the Loop it wasn't so bad till we got to Wacker Drive and ran into the cross-stream. The driver was a good one and he made it to the hotel fifteen minutes before my date with Larry. I asked him to wait and Marta and I got out. After a brief hesitation, Sharon got out too and the three of us went into the lobby. We were halfway to the desk when the brunette put a hand on my arm.

"I'm sorry to tag along," she said. "I don't know what to do. If I go back to that room, and the police—"

"Yeah," I said. "If you'll sit down here somewhere, I'll see what I can think of."

She walked away and sat down in a stiff-looking chair against a pillar. Marta had gone ahead and I caught up with her at the desk. She had already begun to register. The clerk was exceedingly polite. When she'd finished writing her name and address, he bowed, almost cracking his nose on the edge of the desk, and said, "Thank you, Miss Sandor. Would you like the same room you had last night?"

Marta had turned away from the desk and I saw her blue eyes wandering over the lobby. They came to rest finally, lingered a moment, then swung back to the clerk.

"No," she said. "Something with twin beds." The clerk was nodding affably when she said, "I guess there'll be two of us in it."

He stiffened in the middle of a nod and his eyes flickered over me. I shook my head.

"Another girl," Marta said.

The clerk seemed less relieved than frustrated. I gathered he was curious about the guy with Marta Sandor.

"Very good, Miss Sandor. You have no luggage?"

"No."

She started to open her purse and the clerk, now a little fussed, hastened to assure her that it wouldn't be necessary to pay in advance. Then he walked off to signal a bell boy and I drew Marta away from the desk.

"Look, honey," I said, "you don't have to worry about this girl. I'll think of something—"

"No, Mac," she said. Her face was tense and strained again. Then, for a few seconds, it relaxed and that secret smile played over it. "I'm jealous," she said. "I couldn't leave you with somebody else—especially such a pretty girl."

Before she reached the end of the sentence, the smile was gone.

"You stayed here last night?" I said.

"Yes. I knew Diana was staying in the apartment. I hadn't told anyone I was coming back. I didn't want to disturb her."

"But you'd had a letter from her."

"Yes, but the letter was so—unfriendly. I called her from the hotel. I thought maybe she was just joking."

"And what did she tell you?"

"She told me—" She hesitated. Her words came slowly and I knew it was hard for her to speak about it. "She told me to stay—out of her life— or she would make trouble for Mr. Krupp and for me."

"And you believed her?"

"I know the lengths she would go to to get her own way."

"Did you see anybody else last night?"

"Only Barney."

"After you talked to Diana?"

"Yes. I told him I thought I ought to have my own place back. Barney said he'd find me another one. When I tried to tell him about Diana's threat—about Mr. Krupp—he just laughed at me. He said he'd take care of Diana and I should stop worrying."

"Barney said *he* would *take care* of Diana?"

"Yes. Barney was always that way. As long as I can remember, Barney made all the decisions."

"Do you know of a place called the House of Jazz?" I asked her.

She nodded slowly.

"On the West Side, near the river," she said. "Barney owns it."

I found a card in my pocket and handed it to her.

"I wish you would stay here till I see you again," I said. "This is my number. I'll be checking in every few minutes."

She put the card in her purse.

I turned and beckoned to Sharon, who came slowly to where we stood. I explained to her that Miss Sandor had offered to share a room with her. She was grateful. There were tears in her eyes as she went away, following the bell boy who had been hovering around.

Marta watched her go. The brunette had covered maybe twenty paces when Marta took a step after her, made a small strangling sound in her throat and said, "No!" But Sharon didn't hear.

"If you don't want—" I began, and stopped when she turned to look at me.

There was a strange sort of horror in her face.

"She made me think of Dinny," she said. "It was like the whole thing —with Dinny—starting all over again!"

"Listen," I said. "Let me get you another room."

"No. I'll be all right now. Really."

She moved away, then returned, stood close to me for a moment, rose on tiptoe and kissed my cheek.

"Thank you for being sweet," she said. "Goodnight, Mac."

"Goodnight," I said, and it was a good thing she left then, because I couldn't think of anything to say.

She walked away, quick and beautiful, across the lobby and I stood watching till she was out of sight. Then I went out and got in the cab and told him to go to the cafe where I was to meet Larry Evans. I dismissed the cab at this point, figuring it was time to change horses before the stream got any rougher.

CHAPTER 22

The late evening rush was nearly over and there were plenty of booths in the joint. This was a place that had started out with big ideas a few years before. Catering to busy executives, it featured a telephone connection in each booth. Now it was a little faded and run down and the clientele had shifted from the executives to their secretaries and flunkies. But they still had the telephone service.

I went through the place hurriedly and found Larry hadn't arrived yet. I found a booth for myself and ordered coffee and a telephone. My service reported five calls, two of which were unimportant. There was a call from Aaron Krupp from two hours before, and because I had seen him since, I passed it. The other calls were from George Keeler at the *Tribune* and from Donovan's office. I tried to get George, who was out. Then I called Donovan's number and got Samuel. His voice was formal and stiff.

"I have a message for you," he said, "from Lieutenant Donovan, a homicide investigator with the Chicago police, Cook County, Illinois."

"I'm braced for it," I said.

"The Lieutenant says to tell you that the sands of time are running out for all private detectives of Scotch descent. He stated that there are warrants out for the apprehension and arrest of a young man named Norman Krupp and a private detective known around town as Mac. He stated further that it is immaterial to him which is picked up first, but that he will deal with each in his own good time, preferably before dawn."

"What are the charges?"

"In the case of Norman Krupp, murder in the first degree. In the case of the private eye—obstruction of justice, accessory after the fact, assault and battery against a police officer, suppression of evidence, breaking and entering, resorting, aggravated assault, assorted traffic violations—shall I continue?"

"Never mind. I ask you to thank the Lieutenant and tell him kindly to go to hell."

"I have your message," he said and hung up.

So Donovan's dander was up. I didn't doubt that he would throw me in the can if he got sore enough. And as long as he was sore enough, it wouldn't do any good to try to explain anything to him. I would have to avoid him as long as possible, which meant I couldn't stay here, or in any other place for long at a time. Samuel would know where I'd called from by the time he hung up.

I dialed Aaron Krupp's number and after a while he came on the line.

"I didn't find very much, Mac," he said.

"If you read the things off," I said, "I'll take them down. I haven't much time."

He started through the assortment. There were half a dozen match covers from night spots and cafes. All but one of them were on the South Side. The sixth was from the House of Jazz. There were several movie ticket stubs and I noted the names of the theaters, most of which also were on the South Side. There were three business cards, one from a chemical company in South Chicago. One was the name of a beauty parlor on Michigan Avenue and the third read: Ben Champlain—Commercial Photographer.

I kept my voice calm, wrote everything down and asked Krupp to call my number in case the boy showed up. I didn't mention that Donovan had a warrant on him. There was enough for the guy to worry about.

As I hung up, Larry Evans slid into the booth across from me, bringing a cup of coffee. I felt better just seeing him. He was big and wide in the shoulders and I knew him to be competent in any situation that called for calculated action. He didn't rattle easily and he wouldn't start a fight if he could find a way to avoid it. He looked tougher than he acted, mostly because of a long scar across his face that ran from under his left eye, across the bridge of his nose and down toward the right side of his jaw.

"Sorry to drag you out in the middle of the night," I said.

"I'm sleepy," he admitted, "but I can use the work."

I sketched out the problem for him and he looked worried.

"There's a lot of ground to cover, Mac."

"I've got this list," I said. "If you'll take the South Side, I'll take the rest and we'll follow them up. You can use a cab to save time. In checking the night spots, you might check all of them in any area where we have one listed. Forget the movie houses; most of them are closed. Also, we'll skip the chemical company."

"What does the kid look like?"

I described him carefully. I showed him the photograph in Peterson's *Wages of Sin* pamphlet—the one showing Norman and Marta Sandor. Larry's eyes widened.

"Who's the doll?" he asked.

"The doll doesn't figure in it," I said. "We're not looking for her."

He was looking at me closely.

"Who else besides us is looking for the boy?"

I had to level with him.

"The cops," I said.

He took a swallow of coffee.

"Is he guilty?"

"To tell you the truth," I said, "I don't know."

He thought about it for a while and then he said, "All right, Mac. You never steered me wrong yet."

"You're clear," I said. "If you find the boy, all you have to do is stick with him till you hear from me. If the cops should move him, let them have him, but stick with him. There'll be an attorney in a few minutes."

"How often should I call you?"

"At least every half hour. I'll be checking in. If I leave a message for you to call and you can't get me, don't worry. I'm on the run myself."

A guy came in the front door of the cafe and stood looking around. I didn't recognize the face, but he had city cop written all over him. It was quite a distance from our booth to the door and as I watched, he turned to the cashier's window.

"I'm going out the back way," I said to Larry.

"I'll go to the counter and have another cup of coffee," he said. "Good luck, Mac."

"Likewise," I said.

I had separated the South Side addresses Aaron Krupp had given me from those on the North Side and I tore the paper in two, handed part of it to Larry, along with some expense money, and slid out of the booth. I knew he would handle the cop all right and I was pretty sure they wouldn't take him in, although it was known that he sometimes worked for me. But even a cop would hesitate to try to grab Larry if he had a reasonable story.

There was a partition separating the cafe floor from the kitchen entrance and I went behind it, trying not to hurry. The cop was turning away from the cashier's window as I pushed through an aluminum swinging door into the kitchen. There was a service exit straight ahead in the rear wall and I remembered that it gave on an alley where I could go right to Randolph or left to Monroe. There would be cabs somewhere along Wabash after I got out of the alley.

Nobody in the kitchen spoke to me and I moved a little faster as I approached the exit. A chef with a pot of steaming vegetables in one hand backed away from a stove and I dodged around him. He mumbled under his breath, then got busy with his job and left me alone.

The door was heavy and the knob jammed as I twisted it. I looked back once to see whether the cop had got to the kitchen, but nobody came in except a couple of waiters and a bus boy. I forced myself to take time to work the knob, then put my shoulder against the door and pushed. It opened and I went outside, past a row of garbage cans into the alley. The blank walls of the buildings fronting on Wabash shut out the street lights and it was dark in the alley. I turned to my right, heading for Randolph, and came abreast of a recessed doorway in the rear of the next building.

A guy stepped out of it and a quiet voice said, "All right, shamus."

I stopped, because there wasn't any use trying to run.

"Hello, copper," I said.

The guy was Donovan.

CHAPTER 23

I tried to read his face as we stood there in the dark.

"I got your message," I said. "I trust you got mine."

"I did, I did."

"So where do we go from here?"

"Son, you ought to know."

There was no way in the world for me to tell what he was thinking. The only thing I knew surely was that if I should try to walk away from him, he would stop me, with a sap if necessary.

"Personally," I said, "I thought I'd take in a little hot music."

"You did now?"

Donovan took off his hat, scratched the back of his head and jammed the hat back on.

"Shamus," he said, "I don't know. When I walked into that lady's room on Ontario and found Robinson laid out, I figured I was closing in. It takes a desperate man to slug a cop that way. When I found out it was you, I couldn't figure out what got you so desperate."

"I don't have to be desperate to slug Robinson."

"I started piecin' things together. I already knew you was workin' for Norman Krupp—"

"No," I said.

"All right. Then for the kid's old man, old Aaron Krupp."

I kept quiet.

"Robinson asked you to hand over a book you was carryin' when he found you with that broad at the girl's place—"

"She's no broad."

"Whatever you say. It don't really matter about the book—which must of had pictures in it. I had already found a mess of pictures in the dead lady's apartment. I'd like to see whether you found any new ones, but we can come to that later."

"You've been busier than I thought," I said.

"Then I got some other things on the Krupp kid. I went out to his place to talk to him. He wasn't home. He didn't get home."

"So," I said.

"So there's three things I want to know from you; Number One: where is Norman Krupp? Number Two: what's the connection with that blonde you been trailin' along with tonight? Number Three: Who is the other dame, the dark one? I'll find out sooner or later, but I'd like to hear it from you first."

I let him wait a minute and then I said, "Come over in the light, so you can watch me tell you."

"O. K., son," he said, "but remember—I taught you every trick you know, and I've known 'em a lot longer."

I backed away toward the door of the cafe where light spilled through the frosted glass panel. Donovan came along, facing me. I turned my head into the light.

"Sometimes, Lieutenant," I said, "I've refused to answer you, because of a client; and sometimes I haven't always told you everything I knew—for the same reason. But whenever I told you anything, it was the truth. I never lied to you."

There was a dangerous undercurrent in his tone when he said, "No speeches. Just answer the questions."

"That's what I'm about to do. Number One: I don't have any idea where Norman Krupp is. Number Two: I don't know where either of the girls fit in. But I was about to find out when you interrupted me. If you think I can do it while I stand here with you, then all right."

"Don't talk snotty to me."

"Take it easy, copper."

There was some silence then, while Donovan fought to hold himself in and I waited for the right moment to make my next suggestion. I heard him exhale a long, drawn-out breath and figured this moment was as good as any.

"I am about to visit a place called the House of Jazz," I said. "It seems to be where you go if you are a model out of a job."

He had a hard time over it. It had begun to look as if I were pushing for my own way and he was in no mood to take that. But what I had told him was the truth. I have never lied to him and on all the cases we had ever been in together I had been lucky enough to turn up on his side of the fence. But there was not much sentimentality in Donovan and his job always came first. Thinking back over the last few hours, I couldn't remember having taken any undue advantage of him.

I guess he was thinking back too, because pretty soon he shrugged his thick shoulders, took off his hat, jammed it on again, and said, "I'll go along for a while, Mac. But watch your step."

"Shall we call a cab?"

"I can't afford to ride in cabs. We'll use the city car."

I thought he meant streetcar and was about to protest when I saw that he had signaled with a small flashlight into the alley. Headlights went on nearby and Donovan's car and driver pulled in beside us. Donovan opened the back door and I got in.

"Where is the place?" Donovan asked.

I told him and he told the driver. We left the alley, worked into the traffic and headed north toward the Michigan Avenue bridge. I sat quietly beside Donovan, waiting. I waited a long time before he began to talk.

"Evidence," he said. "That's all I've got to work with. What is evidence? Fingerprints. Hair. Skin. Pictures."

He sounded like a lecture on criminal investigation. My mind wanted to skip it, to get back to Marta Sandor and a time when this would be over and settled. But I listened to Donovan.

"I've got the evidence," he went on. "Fingerprints—Norman Krupp's —all over the place. Especially on a highball glass in the kitchen and on the neck of a whisky bottle, which is in the lab. Hair—like the hair that grows on a man's hands, on one of them pillows.

"The pillows were tough. You couldn't see nothing on them wild patterns. But the boys found some. Also a broken fingernail. There was lipstick on the pillow too. The one in the middle. Did you see that, shamus? Don't tell me. I don't want to be disappointed."

I put my hand in my pocket and felt the silver chain I'd found on the rug, inscribed to Barney Sorelle. I wished I had left it where I'd found it. Maybe I would have a chance to put it back.

Donovan went on talking.

"Then there was the pictures. Real gay pictures, of Norman Krupp. And the dead girl. How do you think them pictures would look in the newspapers? A fancy woman and the son of a big storekeeper like Aaron Krupp?"

"The papers don't print pictures like that."

"All right," he said, "but sometimes a man will pay a big price just to make sure."

"Did Norman Krupp pay the price?"

There was a pause. Then Donovan said, "I don't say he did. But the day before yesterday he had a savings account with five thousand dollars in it. Yesterday, there was only five hundred left. There's forty-five hundred bucks that went someplace."

"Maybe he bought a new car."

"I thought of that. But he just bought a new car the week before."

"A house?"

"What would a college boy want with a house?"

I didn't know.

"If he bought the pictures," I said, "he would have picked them up. There wouldn't have been any left for you to find."

"The ones I found were hid," Donovan said. "He must have bought some others."

"Then I don't see that he had any reason left to kill her."

Donovan looked at me.

"I didn't say he killed her. I say I've got enough evidence to bring him in. The rest is up to the jury."

"If the prosecutor can't prove she blackmailed him, then he can't prove a motive for murder."

"My job don't have nothing to do with the prosecutor."

He was in a sour mood all right and there wasn't much point in talking to him. He didn't say any more himself until we pulled up in front of the House of Jazz. There was a faded canopy running from the door to the curb and the police car stopped where it would be convenient for Donovan to step out under the canopy. There were bright lights on the front of the building, with showcards advertising the current talent. I didn't recognize any of the names.

We climbed out of the car and there was a doorman. He started our way, saw the police car, turned and went back inside. I looked at Donovan.

"Great," I said. "If there was anybody in there we might be looking for, he'll have plenty of time to go out the back way."

"Shut up," Donovan said. "The only reason I came here was to keep an eye on you."

I gave him what tried to be a disgusted glance and turned back toward the car.

"I guess you might as well pinch me," I said. "I don't see much ahead here."

He put a hand on my arm heavily.

"I'm tryin' to be patient," he said. "Let's say I already pinched you. But we'll drop in here first, for a quick drink."

So that round ended in a draw. I turned back to the club entrance and Donovan came along behind me. The doorman had reappeared and held the glass door open for us without comment.

Inside, a throb of hot music struck us and cigarette smoke was thick in the air. The lights were much dimmer than was legal and it was hard to find our way through the closely packed tables. Donovan was mumbling between his teeth.

"Goddam dive," he said. "I ought to call the vice department. Where's the manager? Tell him to get some lights on in here."

"You tell him," I said. "You're the big cop around here."

"Shut up," he said.

A cigarette girl brushed past us, wearing a costume so brief she might as well have left it off. Donovan grabbed her arm.

"Listen, girlie," he said. "Where's the boss?"

She got ready to let him have it, then took another look and gave in. I guessed everybody had been tipped off by now.

"He's over at the cashier's window," she said, "and take your dirty hand off me, copper."

She was pretty nasty about it and I held my breath, but Donovan let it pass. He walked away toward the cashier's window and I waited. I had a hunch that if I tried to get away, he'd blow a whistle or something.

I watched him gesturing at the manager and the manager gesturing back, and then the manager went away somewhere and by the time Donovan got back to me the lights were brighter.

"One favor you could do me," I said. "Try not to let anybody know we're together."

"The only favor I feel like doin' you now," he said, "is with the back of my hand."

"O. K.," I said. "You want to mix it up now in front of all these people? Or shall we step outside?"

He glared at me for a minute and I glared back. Then slowly, one corner of his mouth twitched and he began to grin at me. It was like when the sun breaks through a stormy sky. You can expect more clouds, but the break feels good.

"I'll say this, Mac," he said. "You're tough and you're smart If you could only learn to keep out of trouble—"

"I'll watch me and you watch you," I said.

"Then all right," he said. "Let's sit down."

The joint was pretty full and it took a while to find an empty table. When we did, it was off in a corner and Donovan could barely squeeze himself into the chair. It was one of those little round cocktail tables and the waitress was standing over us before we had really got settled. We ordered a couple of bottles of beer and she said they were out of beer. Donovan shoved his badge at her and she said she'd take another look. Pretty soon she came back with the beer.

"Goddam clip joints," Donovan grumbled. "Ought to close 'em all up."

"What about the unemployment?" I said.

He didn't answer.

The only adequate light in the place was on the bandstand and even there the cloud of smoke was so thick you couldn't be sure what you were looking at. There was a small Negro combination giving out with a steady, throbbing beat in a number that seemed endless. In swing fashion, the musicians took turns performing variations on whatever the theme was, and the beat went on and on, never changing, like a heavy, distant pulse. The customers were mostly young, with more boys than girls and they were in various stages of intoxication—whether from liquor or the music, I couldn't be sure. Now and then one or more of them would get up from where they were sitting and go into a kind of frenzied movement that might have been dancing. At these times, they would usually set up a chant to match the drumbeat rhythm, shouting, "Go! Go! Go!"

Donovan sat with his head in his hands.

"What's goin' on here?" he said.

"This is the new music," I said. "Maybe you're getting old."

"Is that right now?"

I wanted to make a phone call to check with Larry Evans, and another to Marta, but I couldn't tell whether Donovan was in a mood to let me go.

I felt a hand on my shoulder and stiffened as I twisted my head to look up. It was a girl dressed in the same brief costume as the cigarette girl, but this one had a flash camera slung over her shoulder. She gave me a load of her white teeth and said, "How about a picture, gentlemen?"

Without looking at Donovan I said, "Sure, Dolly. How long will it take?"

She blinked as I mentioned her name, but held on.

"Just a few minutes."

"Now just a minute, shamus," Donovan said, starting up.

"Sit down," I said. "I've always wanted a picture of you to hang over my garbage can."

"What about your own ugly mug?"

"We'll tear it in two," I said. "You can have half."

He didn't like it, but he sat down again while the girl walked off a ways, fiddled around and make a show of getting us in focus, then pushed the button to make the flash exposure. Donovan was making faces into his beer glass and I beckoned to the girl, who came over to the table again.

"Who owns the concession?" I asked.

"Beg pardon?"

"The photographer—who is it that has the deal to shoot and print the pictures?"

"I really don't know—" Donovan had reached into his pocket and the next thing I knew, his hand came out of it showing his badge. I swore to myself.

"Answer the question, girlie," he said.

She stammered a little and flushed and then she said, "Ben Champlain. He has a studio on the North Side."

"Thanks," I said. "That will be all."

"Is there going to be any trouble?" she said. "I don't want to get mixed up in anything—"

"No trouble," I said. "Run along and get us a print of that, huh?"

I reached out as if to give her a farewell pat and she went quickly.

"Good for you," I said to Donovan. "You getting badge-happy?"

For the first time, he looked a little sheepish. He took a long drink of his beer and I pulled from my pocket the list of names and addresses I'd taken down in the telephone conversation with Aaron Krupp. I told Donovan about the call and where the names came from. I showed him the name of Ben Champlain on the list. Donovan had nothing to say.

"Of course," I said, "by the time we catch up with him, Mr. Champlain will know all about some fat cop asking questions. I thought it was worth a try."

He still said nothing.

"Champlain probably figures he's had enough now, what with you and me—and Robinson. By the way, when are you going to ask Robinson where he got the thousand bucks cash he's carrying?... Not that you'd have a wrong cop on your staff..."

I was being a little hard on him now and I was sorry to have to do it, but I was getting the jitters from being pinned to the wall while he played with me.

He finished his beer, glanced around the room.

"What was it about Robinson?" he said.

"You heard it good."

He pushed his chair back and stood up. When he spoke, his voice was gruff and husky. The set of his jaw was the same as always, but the rest of his face had crumpled like a boy's face when he has just learned he won't be eligible for next week's football game.

"All right, son," he said, "you're on your own. Have a good time."

I watched him walk away across the crowded floor, broad and squat, with his hat low on his head and his big hands swinging at his sides, and I had to fight hard to keep from calling him back.

Because suddenly, for no reason I could have put in words, I was afraid.

CHAPTER 24

I sat there, rigid, for a few minutes, with my back to the room, looking at Donovan's empty chair. Then I got up and moved around the table to sit against the wall. The waitress came and I ordered a shot of good brandy with some water on the side. It felt warm and friendly going down. By the time I had finished it, the girl came back with a photograph in a cheap gray folder. I didn't look at it. I paid her for it and invited her to have a drink.

"I'm not allowed to drink with the customers," she said.

"All right. Where can I find a phone booth?"

"There's a door behind the bandstand. Go through it into the hall. The phone booth is at the far end."

I gave her a tip and she tucked it away somewhere and left.

The musicians were coming back from a break and I had to wait a minute before I could get through the door behind the stand. When I finally made it, I was in a long, narrow corridor with white plaster walls and a cement floor. There was a telephone booth at the far dead end. I passed a couple of closed doors in the outside wall and got into the booth.

I dialed the call service and there were two calls from Larry Evans. He had left a number and I dialed it. I could hear the muffled, primitive-sounding beat from the bandstand while I waited for an answer.

When the circuit opened, I heard music at the other end, but a different type. It had the boomy bass sound of a juke box. I asked for Mr. Evans and the man on the other end said, "Hold on."

I waited a while with the thud of the House of Jazz music in one ear and the different music and rattle of glasses at the other place in the receiver, and standing there in the booth with the door closed, I had a slight touch of claustrophobia. So I began to get scared again, because in my business you can't afford to have claustrophobia.

After what seemed like half an hour, I heard Larry's voice. It sounded good.

"Mac?" he said. "I found him."

"How is he?"

"Drunk."

"Hard to handle?"

118

"Haven't tried. All I can do to keep him in sight."

"Where are you now?"

"Out on the South Side. Some kind of college hangout."

"We're a long way apart. Do you think you can get him away from there?"

"I can try."

I thought about it. My own office was no good, because the cops would be watching it. Likewise Aaron Krupp's house. I could think of no brightly lighted public place where he would be inconspicuous and in the dimly lit joints, the kid would just keep drinking and get more difficult. There was only one place I could think of where the cops would be unlikely to look for Norman Krupp.

"All right," I said to Larry, "I've got a key to an apartment on Walton Place." I gave him the number. "I'll send it by messenger to Tony's place across from my office. You can pick it up there."

"Whatever you say, Mac."

"And call his old man. Tell him we found the boy and he's all right and we'll call him again."

"How soon will you make it to the apartment?"

"It may take some time. You'll have to watch your step around Tony's. If Tony is there and the key hasn't arrived yet, get Tony to let you in the back room."

"O. K.," he said, "and Mac—"

"Yeah."

"The word is out for you. The cabs are getting the flash. You're wanted for questioning."

"Forget it," I said. "It's that bull-headed Irishman—"

"Donovan?"

"Yeah. Thanks, boy and take care of young Krupp. I'll meet you when I can."

"So long, Mac."

He hung up. I hung up too and waited for the dial tone. I dialed the Palmer House and asked for Marta's room number. The phone rang several times and the operator said, "There's no answer."

"Keep trying. Maybe she's asleep."

The phone rang some more. In the tight little booth, the air was getting stale and I could feel the sweat gathering under my hat and around the back of my neck. The beat-beat-beat of the music in the other room was like the repeated tapping of a hammer on the side of my head.

Finally the operator broke in again.

"Let me have the clerk," I said.

119

The clerk came on and I asked whether the girl in Room 613 had checked out. It took him forever to find out and when he came back on again he said, "No, sir."

"Have you seen her leave?" I asked. "A small girl, blonde, with a patent leather bag—"

His voice was cool and professional.

"I can't say, sir," he said, "and even if I did know, I don't think I could give you that information."

"Listen," I said, "don't make it hard for me—"

"I'm sorry, sir," he said and hung up.

I replaced the receiver and jerked the door of the booth open, sucking in gasps of air. My hand was shaking as I took off my hat, rubbed the back of my neck and replaced the hat.

If she left the hotel, I thought, she must have gone home.

I went back to the phone and realized I didn't know the number at her apartment. I went through the directory but found no listing. I dialed Donovan's office and got Samuel.

"Mac," I said. "Do me a favor."

"The favors have all been done," he said.

"I need the phone number at Marta Sandor's apartment. I need it bad."

After a moment, Samuel said, "I hate to say this, but the Lieutenant is very unhappy—"

"Look, Samuel. I've just been with Donovan. Everything's all right. Just let me have the number."

"You know better, Mac. I've got a job here. In eight more years I can retire—" I swore at him, loud and fast. When I stopped there was quite a bit of silence.

"I'm sorry," he said.

"Everybody's so goddam sorry," I said bitterly.

Then I pulled myself up and took a long breath.

"I have a message for you and the Lieutenant," I said.

"Very good. I have a pencil."

"I realize it's not a very big ball for two such potbellied flatfeet as yourselves, but I do wish to Christ you would at least try to get on it."

I slammed the receiver onto the hook and did some more heavy breathing. All it did for me was to dry out my throat. I coughed a little, counted slowly to ten and stepped out of the booth. I walked about six feet along the corridor and stopped.

Coming toward me from the other end were three guys, two tall ones and a short, squatty one. The two tall ones didn't really matter. The short, squatty one was in the middle and his name was Barney Sorelle.

CHAPTER 25

As they approached I recognized Bronk and his sidekick, Alex. Sorelle's two throwbacks, I thought. They weren't taking any chances; Bronk had a gun in his hand. I stood still, waiting. They stopped, facing me, three abreast. Sorelle's face was distorted and it took a while for him to get any words out.

"You get around some, don't you, shamus?" he said.

I didn't say anything.

Let him do his own talking, I thought. Maybe if he would talk for a while it would take some of that murder out of his face. I remembered having helped to put it there, but it was no time for vain regrets.

"You said I was out of date," he said next. "Maybe a little old-fashioned treatment is what you need."

Again I kept quiet. But it only made him hot. Standing there, flanked by his two pet monkeys, he reached up and slapped the side of my face with the back of his hand. I felt the big diamond ring cut into the flesh over the pain of the blow. Inside my head a faint singing began. I had heard it before and it was a dull kind of music.

You have to keep calm, Mac, I said to myself. You have to hold on. Mixing it up now would be the finish and you're not through yet.

"So we're even," I said. "Maybe things could be talked over."

The words crawled over my tongue like worms.

"Oh—" he said, "not so tough now, shamus?"

He hit me again. I barely felt it, but the red-hot needle of my temper flared in my stomach. I felt my hand clench and mentally pried my fingers open.

"Take it easy, Sorelle," I said. "It's a small world."

"Yeah," he said. "Right in here. A very small world."

He was holding his slapping hand in front of him, his fingers twitching a little, and I thought, Not again, goddam it! If he does it again I won't be able to hold on.

"I want nothing from you," I said. "If you want something from me, tell me what it is. I'll see if I've got it."

He had the look on his face a man gets when he's brought somebody to heel. It's not a pleasant look.

"I've got plenty of time," he said. "I waited till your fat cop friend left, I can wait a while longer."

"Shall we sit down?" I said.

"Sure," he said. "Right this way."

He stepped aside and gave me an exaggerated bow.

"My private office," he said. "The first door on your left. Don't bother trying to make a break. My boys may be old-fashioned, but they shoot pretty good."

I went past him, the two bodyguards pivoting with me as I moved, and on down the corridor to the first door. There might be a break here—if the door was unlocked and I could get through it fast enough, I'd have my own gun out by the time they came through.

But the door was locked and I stood and waited for Sorelle to come along and put the key in it. When it swung open, I started in, but he put his hand on my chest and shoved me back.

"Take it easy," he said. "There's plenty of room for everybody."

He walked into the office and I stood, waiting. The two gorillas were behind me and suddenly one of them planted a hand between my shoulder blades and pushed. I fell forward into the room and rolled to one side, expecting Sorelle to kick me. My neck had snapped with the sudden push and I lay still for a moment, wishing one of them would slug me hard enough to knock me out and get it over with.

How many mistakes can a man make, I wondered, and still get along in life?

I had made the first one when I hit Sorelle in my office and another when I told George Keeler about Sorelle having a key to the dead girl's apartment. But I was horse trading with George. I had to tell him.

Sorelle's foot rubbed across my ribs.

"Get up," he said. "Make yourself comfortable."

I got my knees under me, twisting my head slowly to relieve the kink in my neck. I guess I didn't move fast enough to suit him, because he let me have it with the foot again in the shoulder. I straightened up and backed away. They were lined up again, three abreast, and Bronk still had the gun in his hand.

"I think he's got a gun," Bronk said brightly.

"Sure he has," Sorelle said. "You want to get close enough to take it away from him?"

Bronk stood still. We were in the middle of a spacious office, with unfinished brick walls, some overstuffed furniture and a row of filing cabinets along one wall. Light came from a green-shaded overhead fixture hanging over a big desk that slanted across the floor. There was a wreath of fresh flowers on a wire stand on one corner of the desk. The arrangement spelled out HAPPY BIRTHDAY BARNEY.

On the far side of the desk was a high-backed leather swivel chair. Sorelle walked around and sat down in it. I noticed that I could no longer hear the beat of the music from the other room. Great. So nobody outside could hear what went on in here either. Not that there was anybody who, hearing anything, would care.

Sorelle glanced at Bronk and said, "Ask him to sit down."

I knew how he would ask, and I backed away some more, felt the backs of my knees come up against the edge of a seat. I sat down on it and it turned out to be a davenport. The upholstery was torn and some of the stuffing showed through near my left knee.

Bronk, the boy with the speedball brain, kept advancing, but Sorelle called him off.

"The shamus is doing better," he said. "Leave him alone." Bronk stopped. The other one, Alex, just stood around with his shoulders slumping. I noticed there was a fresh cut on the back of his hand and every once in a while he would pull a handkerchief from his pocket and dab at it.

Sorelle leaned back in his chair and closed his eyes. His fat fingers were drumming softly on the desk top.

"All day," he said, "nosey newspaper guys, cops, come around and bother me. Why, shamus?"

"I wouldn't know," I said. "Everybody has to live his own life."

"Yeah. So why should you try to live mine too?"

"I beg your pardon?"

"I will explain. You got a client—a young rich kid. To keep his name out of the newspapers, you throw mine in."

He had me pretty well pinned down.

"I figured you were used to it," I said.

"I don't like it. I got all the publicity I can handle."

"Is that what you want from me?" I said. "An apology?"

His sleepy eyes opened and held me for a moment.

"That wouldn't help much, would it?"

"I couldn't say."

He closed his eyes again.

"You have got a reputation around town," he said. "Untouchable. Nobody lays a finger on Mac. Is that right? Nobody touches. If somebody does, he gets it back. If not from Mac, then from his cop pal, Donovan. Am I right?"

"I try to take care of myself," I said.

"A boy like you needs a lesson maybe. Too much reputation—that's not good."

"If you mean what I think you mean," I said, "it's murder."

"Maybe not."

"If you'd thought of working me over, you might as well forget it. You know damned well I'd be back."

"More big talk?"

"Sure big talk. If you're thinking of rough stuff, you better think about finishing me off, because I promise you I'll never forget."

It was big talk in a way, but it was true talk too, and I hoped he would understand that I meant it.

"I wasn't thinking of working you over," he said. "It would be a pleasure, but not practical. I believe you all right."

"Good. Then let's get the conversation over with so I can be on my way."

"Relax, shamus," he said. "You haven't got anywhere to go anymore."

Something in the way he said it got me by the throat. I stared at him across the room and I looked at the fresh cut on the back of Alex's hand. A red haze began to form and I blinked my eyes to erase it. Sorelle smiled sadly.

"I like to get along with everybody," he said. "But sometimes, people have to have lessons. I had to give a lesson tonight. I hated to do it—she was always such a pretty girl."

I stood up slowly, bracing the backs of my legs against the davenport. My hands were shaking and I knew they wouldn't be able to brush away the red haze. Sorelle was watching me closely and suddenly he nodded at Bronk.

"Ask the shamus to sit down," he said.

Bronk was close to me this time, he still had the gun, and his mind still worked on schedule. He took a step and because the gun was in his right hand, he decided to use it as a club. Which was fine, because when he raised it to slug me, it was no longer pointing at me. Also, twisting to get at me threw him off balance.

I hit him so hard I thought my hand had broken. I'd caught the side of his head and he dropped the gun and slid all the way to Sorelle's desk before he stopped and lay still. His partner had moved in right away, but I got hold of the gun and jammed it hard into his belly when he reached for me. He sat down, holding onto himself and I backed toward the door, covering Sorelle, who now stood behind his desk, both hands flat on its top.

The one on the floor started to get up and I said, "Don't try it. Believe me, I'll let you have it."

He stopped moving, looked up at Sorelle. The pudgy one was looking at me with the face-saving grin and he didn't look worried.

"Let him go," he said. "I wanted him to sweat a while longer, but there's plenty of time."

I got my hand on the doorknob and twisted it, still covering them with the gun.

"Like you said, shamus," Sorelle said, "we're even. I can't kill you and you can't kill me. But no friend of yours will ever be safe. You got a long life of sweat ahead of you."

"You're wrong on one point," I said. "I can kill you. I can hang the murder of Diana Peterson on you. And your sister will help me. I'll have plenty of help. I've got the evidence in my pocket. Happy birthday, Barney."

I backed through the door, slamming it shut, and I kept the gun out in my hand while I backed down the corridor and found the door leading into the club behind the bandstand. After I got out there I dropped the gun into my pocket and made my way among the tight-packed tables to the front door and outside. Nobody spoke to me, which was just as well.

CHAPTER 26

There were three cabs parked in front of the place and I got in the nearest one. I told him to get me to a phone booth in a hurry and he did it, pulling up on a dark street where a public booth stood near a closed filling station. I told him to keep the motor running and went to make my call.

I dialed the Palmer House, asked for her room number and waited while the phone rang twelve times. There was no answer.

I returned to the cab and crawled into the back seat. I gave the driver the address on Walton Place. He started off and made a couple of wrong turns and I swore at him. He pulled into the curb and looked back at me.

"If you want to get out now," he said, "maybe there'll be another cab along after a while."

"All right," I said, "I'll try to contain myself."

It looked as if I'd eat plenty of crow before morning. I had done it before, but it had never tasted worse than now.

He went along pretty well after that and found a place to park in front of the building. When I asked him to wait, he said, "O. K., tough guy."

I let it pass. There were so many things you had to let pass.

I went through the foyer quickly and got in the elevator. The place was quiet, as usual, and I saw nobody on the way up, nor in the corridor as I walked to the apartment door. I found the key I'd used earlier to let myself in and there were no lights on inside. I found the switch and made light.

She wasn't anywhere in the living room. The white shag rug was smooth and undisturbed. The pillows lay on the davenport where I had left them. I went on into the bedroom, glancing into the bath as I passed, and found nobody. I came out again, crossed the living room, went through the dinette and into the kitchen. I switched on the light in there.

I had been tense and shaky until then, driving myself inside, but suddenly I went limp in the middle, as if the breath had been kicked out of me. Sweat broke out on my face and I made my way slowly to the big white refrigerator and I leaned against it and stared across the narrow room, seeing nothing, fighting to get my nerves tight again.

I stared for a long time and I guess I talked a certain amount too, though I can no longer remember the words. But finally I moved again, stiffly, and reached for the empty highball glass on the shelf. I picked it up and turned it round and round in my hand and then I raised it over my head and threw it at the wall as hard as I could throw.

The sudden effort and the crashing sound of the glass tightened me up again and I went out of the kitchen and back to the living room. I hung around in there for a few minutes to no purpose and finally I went back downstairs to the waiting cab. As we drifted around the corner, heading for my office, I saw the stocky, wide silhouette of Donovan, under the street light, looking up toward the apartment building.

I asked the driver to stop, opened the door on the curb side and called quietly to Donovan. He looked carefully to make sure who had called him, then moved slowly to the cab. He leaned heavily on the open door, looking at me, saying nothing.

"I can't handle it alone," I said. "I know too much, but still not enough."

Donovan's big face was gray and flat in the dingy light.

"What do you know," he said, "that I don't?"

"Barney Sorelle's sister came back to town."

"The blonde," he said. "I know that. Registered at the Palmer House."

"Sorelle was hot on the dead girl—for a while anyway. He put her up in his sister's apartment. The dead girl was a bitch. Under Sorelle's protection, she kicked the sister around for a long time. She was used to being kicked around. Her brother—"

"Uh-huh."

"The dead brunette was a real no-good."

"Like I said," Donovan said, "she tried to blackmail Norman Krupp."

"Yes. Also Norman's old man."

There was a pause.

"Aaron?" Donovan said slowly. "That I didn't know."

"Sorelle's sister was very fond of Aaron Krupp. She got wind of the deal and came back."

"How was it to be done?"

"Faked photos. Publicity shots of Marta Sandor and Aaron Krupp, taken at public affairs. The Peterson girl must have worked it out with Champlain, the photographer."

"So?" Donovan's voice was completely neutral.

"Champlain is tied up with Sorelle on some kind of mail-order deal. Dirty pictures. Two of Sorelle's boys cleared out the room on Ontario where the Peterson girl officially lived. They took the stuff to Champlain's place."

"Sorelle wouldn't fool with blackmail."

"All right. But he wouldn't like it if one of his boys—or girls—fooled with it on the side."

Donovan shifted his position slightly. It was a sign of acute interest, though his face showed nothing.

"When Marta Sandor went to her brother about the blackmail threat against Krupp, he said to her, quote: 'I will *take care* of Diana Peterson.'"

Donovan said nothing and after a while I said, "Somebody 'took care' of Diana Peterson, as we know."

"Uh-huh. Norman Krupp?"

"Or Sorelle. Or Champlain, when he was afraid the girl would rat on him to Barney."

There was another pause and I said, "The case is still open, Donovan. You want to look into it a little deeper?"

The street light glinted dully from the whites of his eyes as he turned to look me in the face.

"Will you turn Norman Krupp over to me, when I ask for him?"

"Yes."

"Where is Sorelle's sister now?"

"I don't know. I hoped you could find her. Big brother decided to really kick her around. I don't know where."

"Where are you going?"

"To see a girl. Then to Champlain's."

Donovan backed away from the cab door till it swung clear.

"All right, Mac," he said. "Watch your step."

I reached for the door handle.

"How about Robinson?" I said.

"I sent him home," Donovan said. "He don't work for me any more."

"So long, copper," I said, pulling the door to.

Donovan walked off, squat and heavy footed, his thick shoulders sagging a little under his tight coat.

CHAPTER 27

I left the cab in front of my office and got in my own car. I drove fast by side streets to Ontario, turned back toward Michigan and pulled up in front of the Apollo Hotel. Most of its windows were dark.

From the dreary foyer I went up the stairs two steps at a time and I was beginning to pant when I reached the room where we'd been interrupted by Sharon, later by Robinson. There was no light showing under the door, but I knocked, waited five or ten seconds and knocked again. Pretty soon I heard the squeak of the couch springs and then Sharon's voice, flat and dull from the dark room.

"Go away. Leave me alone."

"It's Mac," I said. I tried the knob and the door was locked. "If you don't open it, I'll knock it down."

There was more squeaking, light footsteps, the door latch clicked and the footsteps retreated quickly. I pushed through the door.

"May I turn on the light?" I said.

"If you have to."

I pawed at the wall till I found the switch and snapped on the light. Sharon sat on the edge of the couch, still fully dressed, her feet on the floor, her knees squeezed tightly together, her shoulders hunched forward a little. She looked sick. There were no marks on her, but she was pale and she looked sick the way you do after too much to drink. She wouldn't look at me, but held her head twisted to one side. Now and then she would tremble all over, as from a chill.

I propped my back against the door. I was afraid to ask what I had to ask.

"What happened?"

It was quite a long time before she answered. When she made up her mind to go ahead I saw a convulsive movement in her throat and thought she was going to be sick, but she held onto herself.

"Two men came to the room. We hadn't gone to bed. It was a few minutes after you left. They were big, tough looking men. They were surprised to see me. They told Miss Sandor to come with them—to see somebody. Then they talked it over and decided I'd better go along too."

She paused, gulped a couple of times, and went on with it.

"They took us downstairs and out through a back door. There was a big car waiting, with another man in the back seat. Miss Sandor got in the back and I sat in front between the two men. There was a glass partition between the front and back and I couldn't hear anything that was said in the back. The men in front didn't say anything to me. I asked where we were going but they wouldn't answer.

"We drove a long way. I don't know where. I don't know the city. When we stopped we were in some kind of alley. Just brick walls and a rough street.

"They made me get out of the car and one of the men held me by the arm. Miss Sandor was standing against a wall and the man from the back seat was walking back and forth in front of her. He was short and fat looking. He would ask a question and Miss Sandor would answer him. He didn't like the answers. Finally he said something to one of the other men —the biggest one, and he went to her and—" She broke down then. Her shoulders began to shake and she sobbed, quietly but with pain. I went to the kitchen alcove, found a glass and filled it with cold water. When I got back to her with it, the sobbing had eased up.

"All right," I said. "He beat her up. You don't have to describe it. How did you get home?"

"I couldn't stand it. I was scared and desperate. I jerked away from the one who was holding me and—I ran away."

"Smart girl."

"He came after me and I ran into some kind of shed and hid behind some barrels. He looked around for a while and then went away. I walked to a street and kept walking till a taxi came along."

"You didn't look for a cop?"

"Yes. There weren't any."

"Did you tell the cab driver?"

"I told him. But he said he couldn't get mixed up in it. He said if we found a cop, we could tell him. But we never saw a cop and by then I couldn't remember where it had happened. When I got home, it took every penny I had for the fare. I couldn't even make a phone call. I was afraid to go out on the street."

Her sobbing had nearly stopped. Once in a while she would tremble, but her eyes were dry and her voice rasped slightly when she spoke.

"Try to remember what was said," I asked her. "When the fat man was questioning her. What did he say?"

"I can't remember."

"Please try."

"Once—he said, 'You had money, everything you needed. Why did you come back?'...And Miss Sandor said, 'I wanted my own name and my own home. I wanted to protect my own friends.'

"And after a while he said, 'You know why we're here? You know what's going to happen?' And she said, 'I can guess. It's the same thing that's happened all my life, Barney—in different ways. Only I didn't realize it till yesterday.' And then he said something about you—about her hanging around with a—" She hesitated.

"With a what?"

"With a—dirty—"

"Dirty shamus?"

"Yes."

"Don't worry about it. It's only a dirty word if you mean it that way."

I went to the door. With my hand on the knob I turned back to look at her.

"The fat one, that had her beat up," I said, "is the guy you'll be working for if you go ahead with Peterson."

She put her face in her hands. I opened the door. The couch springs groaned suddenly and she was across the room, her hands clutching at me.

"Mac—what will I do? Where can I go?"

"Back home."

"But now. Tonight. If they came back—?"

I led her back to the couch. The gun I'd picked up in Sorelle's office at the House of Jazz was heavy in my coat pocket.

"Ever shoot a gun?" I asked her.

"A little. My brother had one—" I gave her the gun, showed her how it worked.

"Keep your door locked. If anybody comes, stay on the couch and ask who it is. It it's a telegram, tell him to push it under the door. If it's the manager, ask him his business and tell him to see you in the morning. If he says it's a cop, ask him to push his badge or I. D card under the door." I described what the I. D card should look like. "If it's somebody else and they try to break down the door, then get the gun ready and if they come in, shoot. At the same time, start screaming as loud as you can."

She held the gun in her cupped hands, staring at it. I was closing the door from the outside when she said quietly, "Thank you, Mac."

I waited for a minute outside till I heard her check the lock on the door. Then I went down to my car. I got away fast and there was no problem now about working into the northbound traffic. As I passed my own street I glanced down toward Tony's, remembering that I'd promised to meet Larry and Norman Krupp there. But I wouldn't have time now. Larry and Norman would have to wait.

It was good that the traffic was light, but I kept within the speed limits after I turned west and circled a couple of blocks, searching for Ben

Champlain's studio. When I found it I parked on the street in front. The front door was locked, as I had expected. I walked west along the street and turned into the alley under the sign that read PARKING IN REAR. I followed it to the back. Light came from the row of windows along the back of the building. The heavy steel door was locked. I stepped back from it and took out my gun, hesitated, thinking about it, and then flattened against the wall beside the door at the sound of footsteps inside. I waited, feeling silly about the gun, while the doorknob grated and the heavy panel ground open. Champlain stepped outside, lighting a cigarette as he came, leaving the door ajar. He turned away from me as he left the doorway and I moved in behind him and spoke quietly.

"My gun is quick, as the boy says. Hold still."

I guess he was nervous, because he didn't hold still. He wheeled around and went for my gun. There were only eight feet of space between us and we covered it in one stride apiece. I feinted with the gun to his left, then snapped his head back with a left hook. He fell, rolled over on the cement and started back up. I grabbed the back of his shirt to help him. On his feet again, with my gun where he could see it and my hand twisting into his back, he stood still.

"Into the studio," I said.

I gave him a push and he walked along all right in front of me, through the big door into the acrid odors of the photographic lab and bright light. There were long assembly tables against the wall on my right and a skinny guy in his undershirt was feeding wet prints into the slowly revolving drums of two print driers. He had his back to the door and paid no attention to the sound we made entering. After a moment he turned casually to glance over his shoulder, glanced away and then back swiftly in a hard double-take. I felt Champlain shrug under his shirt.

"What the hell?" the skinny one said.

Champlain shrugged again and I pushed him away from me toward the other one, who didn't move to help him, but stood with a handful of dripping prints, staring. All of a sudden he dropped them to the floor, walked sideways to a portable wardrobe and took out a shirt and coat. Without bothering to put them on, he skirted around us warily and backed to the door.

"This is no place for me," he said, and disappeared.

A moment later I heard a car motor start and the squeak of tires as he got away.

Champlain was looking at me with a poker face.

"What's all the excitement?" he said.

"The two boxes Bronk and Alex brought out here. Where are they?"

"I don't know—" I took a step toward him and he threw a hand up and backed away.

"Let's not get messy about it. Take me to the boxes. I'm all out of time."

He saw that I meant it. He turned and walked into the corridor that ran beside the wall of the warehouse next door. At the big double steel doors I saw there was light on the other side. Champlain hesitated, glanced back at me, then lifted a bolt and pushed the door open.

Inside the warehouse, I saw that the lighted area was small and concentrated near the door. The huge, high-ceilinged room stretched into shadow on both sides and ahead of me. There was block-and-tackle equipment and the shadow of an overhead crane at the far end. High on the wall to my left was a catwalk with an iron railing. Sliding doors below the catwalk probably opened onto rear loading platforms. Hanging near the catwalk were heavy ropes on pulleys, some with counterweights attached. I gathered the place had been converted for moving heavy equipment after the dress shop closed down.

The section near the door, the lighted part, had been arranged for the mail-order business and there were long tables like those in the lab and stacks of envelopes, wrapping paper and other mailing supplies. The tables were in two long rows with a wide alley between. The light hung from the ceiling over the center of the alley. There were chairs here and there along the tables and in one of the chairs sat Carl Peterson. He lifted his head and turned slowly to look at us when Champlain and I walked in.

CHAPTER 28

He had been sitting with his long head resting on the palm of one hand, looking at a pile of pamphlets and pictures. Two cartons sat on the table near his elbow. He wore the white suspenders over a blue denim shirt and looked the same as when I had seen him in his own room on LaSalle Street.

I prodded Champlain and we walked over to the table, close to Peterson, who said nothing, but watched us with his mournful eyes.

"I hope you've got it well sorted out," I said, "because if there are any pictures in there of Marta Sandor—the real Marta Sandor—I want them. Including the ones in which her face has been substituted for Diana Peterson's."

Peterson's eyes moved slowly to Champlain.

"Who is this?" he said.

"You know damn well who this is," I said. "I just came from Sharon—remember her?—and she knows about you now too."

He just looked at me, insolently, detached.

"I don't know what you're talking about—"

"I understand," I said, "that you peddle your wares by mail."

"I use whatever opportunities present themselves to spread the true word," he said. "The world is weary of evil. There are those who would be saved—"

"I've heard all this. I wonder—could it be possible that you are playing it straight?"

I glanced over his head at Champlain, whose eyes flicked from mine to Peterson's, then back to my face again.

"Let's get to the girl," I said, "the dead one—also, the one who is still alive."

"Young man," Peterson said, "I don't know what you are trying to do —"

"I'm trying to get straightened out. The dead girl was named Diana Peterson."

His thin, bony face didn't budge, but he looked at me coldly out of his deep-set eyes. He looked quite a lot like a spaniel.

"She was not your daughter," I said, "by any woman in this world."

"She was my daughter in a larger sense," he said, "as the women of the world are the daughters of right-thinking men."

"I thought you said yesterday they were children of evil."

"You distort my words."

The edge of my already raveled patience was very ragged. "Look," I said, "I've got no quarrel with religion. I don't make fun of it. But your kind of religion is nothing but fear and hate and revenge—not to mention a come-on for the mail-order smut market."

That hit him somewhere. He started up out of his chair, then sat down again and looked at Champlain.

"What is he saying?" he said.

"Take it easy," Champlain said.

Peterson looked at me.

"I am the vice-president of the Salvation Publishing Company. My only interest is in printing and distributing the message of righteousness —" I'd had too much. I wouldn't have done it except that I'd had too much of everything. I hadn't found Marta. I'd seen the sick fear in Sharon, the worry in Aaron Krupp. I'd seen the dead, naked girl in the beautiful apartment. I'd had all of it, in a very short time. I lifted my left hand and slugged Petersen in the face so that he staggered in his chair and nearly fell out of it.

"Don't give me that phony crap," I said. "You think a girl gets killed for posing for religious pamphlets? You think Barney Sorelle finances a mail-order business to sell the word of God?

"Look, Father Peterson, get wise. They used you to hook them. They send out a little book about the wages of sin. Fine. Couple of pictures, a boy and girl necking. Wind up with a nude girl on a white shag rug. The book says send for more pamphlets. So your job is over. From there on out, it's pictures of naked girls all over the place. Nothing to do with religion. Nothing to do with saving souls."

He rose stiffly from the chair. It was the first time I'd ever seen anything except smugness in his face.

"No—!" he said.

"I say yes. Ask Champlain here. He takes the pictures. It's not too hard to get girls to pose for them—once or twice. But the young, healthy, beautiful ones don't usually like it. They'd rather do something else. So you have to keep changing them all the time and it's a nuisance. But if they can be wangled into it through a nice fatherly type like you—maybe they can be counted on for more pictures. It's for the good of humanity. And on top of that, if Barney Sorelle likes one of them well enough to show her a big time, it's still easier."

He had turned to Champlain, who was backing away from him.

135

"Is this true?" Peterson asked him.

"He's nuts," Champlain said.

"So," I said, "a girl like Diana Peterson comes to town and gets roped in by the nice, fatherly gentleman who all he wants is for her to make some illustrations for religious books. But she falls in with other companions. The big boss likes her. She gets ideas. She begins branching out on her own, with a little help from Mr. Champlain, and pretty soon she gets out of hand. And she gets killed.

"I saw how that happened. I saw it start all over again tonight with a girl named Sharon. But I don't think Sharon will stick around long enough to get killed."

Peterson was rigid now, staring at Champlain.

"If she should stick around," I said, "she will certainly either get killed or suffer something almost as bad. And you would have brought it about, Peterson. Because Barney Sorelle doesn't care about your religion. He only cares about the girls and the money they can make for him.

"I think you know this. If you don't know it, then you are one of our town's most incredible suckers. You are either a dumb stooge or a smart executive. Which is it, Peterson? Do you really think Diana lived in that miserable room on Ontario Street? Didn't you really know that she lived in a fancy apartment on Walton Place that Barney Sorelle stole from his own sister?

"Come on, Peterson. Which is it? Do you work for Sorelle? Or does he work for you?"

I don't think he even heard that last. He was concentrating on Champlain. I guess there must have been some special look on his face which I couldn't see, because all of a sudden Champlain was back-pedaling and then Peterson was going after him, his long arms waving, and Champlain was trying to find a way to hold him off. But Peterson was taller and in spite of Champlain's paunchiness, probably heavier, and pretty soon they were scrabbling around on the cement floor. Neither one was much of a bargain for the fighting ring, so neither could get hurt much, except by accident.

I let them scramble for a while and then I squeezed off with my .38 and heard the slug whine across the floor. That stopped them. They both went stiff and looked at me.

"Break it up," I said. "Put the stuff back in those cartons." I had to threaten them again with the gun before they would climb to their feet and go to the table. Then they picked up the stacks of pamphlets and pictures and dumped them into the cartons.

"Each of you can take one of them," I said, "and we'll carry them out to my car."

They picked up the cartons and I followed them into the corridor and down to the front door. They didn't give me any arguments. They had no words for each other. I still couldn't tell whether Peterson was honestly in the dark about the racket or whether he had just put on a show for my benefit. But I didn't really care either. I didn't even care about the stuff in the cartons any more, but I wanted to give them something to do and I wanted them to worry.

The car keys were in my pocket and I had them lock the car doors. To Peterson I said, "I've got some more business with Champlain inside. I've got no more with you, that I know of. You can run along now, or you can come back in with us. Suit yourself."

He stood there, tall and gaunt, looking at me, then for quite a long time at Champlain, who finally looked away. Then he turned and walked away down the dark street, his shoulders stiff and not moving as he walked, his big hands swinging loosely beside him.

I turned to Champlain.

"Back into the studio," I said, "where you shoot the pictures."

I still had the gun in my hand and I put it away as he turned without a word and started back into the building. Everything went fine till we got into a dark corner behind his front office, with a blank-looking door ahead of us and nothing but white plaster walls on the other side—a narrow, vestibule-like space. Then he turned on me suddenly and we stood close together and he said, "Listen, shamus, you've brought me enough grief for one night. Get the hell out of here."

The quarters were close and the moment was bad. I was surprised that he had so much fight left in him. For a split second he had an advantage over me. I don't think he knew it, but I didn't wait to go into it. I just hit him. I hit him hard in the stomach and he bent and charged me, but it was easy then to push him around in the little cubbyhole we had to move in, and when I had him where I could handle it, with one hand on his throat, pressing his head back against the wall and the other free to slap him when necessary, I said, "Don't try it, Champlain. Just go into your studio quietly. We don't have to fight."

He flailed with his arms some, but then he quieted down and I released him little by little so he could turn and open the door into the studio.

"I've got a picture that needs taking," I said. "Get a camera."

He didn't move.

"What kind?" he said.

"Some kind that doesn't take much time."

The studio was spacious, with a bunch of lights on dollies, a couple of eight by ten view cameras and a few props. On one wall was a high rack of rollers with backdrops and floor coverings. I went over there while

Champlain was finding a camera and sure enough, one of the items on the rack was a white shag rug. I got hold of an edge of it and rolled it out over the floor. Champlain had switched on a couple of flood lamps. The bright light reflected from his bald spot as he turned toward me, holding a battered four by five Graphic. When he saw the rug I'd rolled out, he blinked a little, but made no comment. I found the silver pin and chain with Barney's birthday inscription on it and dropped it onto the rug.

"Shoot that," I said.

He blinked some more and started arranging the lights.

"Try to get it sharp enough so they can read the engraving." I said. "It says, 'Happy Birthday to Barney—from Marta.'"

His eyes danced past me toward the door but he made no move.

"I found it where Marta Sandor was murdered," I said.

"I don't think I can—"

"Then as close as you can get. Hurry up!"

He got on his knees, focused the camera, fiddled some more with one of the lights and aimed it again. After he'd shot it once, he pulled the holder out of the camera, reversed it and shot again.

"That's enough," I said. "Give me the holder."

He hesitated.

"Give it to me," I said. "Sorelle can afford to buy you a new one."

He shrugged, pulled the holder out again and handed it to me. I put it in my pocket. I got my gun out again.

"I'll go out the back way," I said. "You first."

He didn't put up any more objections. He walked out of the studio, into the corridor and I followed him past the still open door to the warehouse mailing room and into the lab. I went past him then, pivoting to face him near the door.

"When you call Sorelle," I said, "you can say I just started building the frame. It won't take long to finish it."

He stood there, still holding the camera, staring at me.

"And by the way," I said, "the cop you paid off today has been busted. Maybe you'd like to tell Sorelle about that too, to explain where the money came from, and where it went."

A telephone rang, somewhere behind me near the door. I backed slowly, feeling with my hand till I found the instrument. I pulled it off the hook and said, "Hello."

The voice was Samuel's, from Donovan's office.

"Mac—?" he said. "Donovan thought I might get you here."

"Yeah?"

"Donovan said you might want to meet him, at the Passavant Hospital."

138

"Donovan and who else?"

"Some girl. A blonde. Donovan said you'd know."

I hung up. Champlain was watching me.

"I'll want to talk to you later," I said. "Hang around—or suit yourself. I'll find you."

He said nothing. I went out the big door, across the parking lot and ran along the alley to the street and my car.

CHAPTER 29

The hospital was only a four-minute walk from my office. I stopped in at Tony's and he told me there were two guys waiting for me in his back room. I went back there. The room was dark and I had only the light that came when the door stood open. Larry was sitting on a straight chair, leaning on a table. I couldn't see the Krupp boy.

"Well, well," Larry said. "The traveler."

"I'm in a hurry," I said. "Where's Krupp?"

"He's lying down. He's been a little sick off and on."

"Norman?" I said into the darkness.

From somewhere in the room he answered me with a groan.

"Listen to me. I've got to go somewhere for a while, with Larry here. I want you to stay here. I'll be back."

Only silence.

"Understand?" I said. "I want you to stay right here. Tony won't let you out, even if you try it, so take it easy till I get back."

Only another groan came back to me.

"How sick is he?" I asked.

"Just in the stomach," Larry said. "How well I remember."

"All right. Let's go."

Larry got up and came with me. Tony was standing just outside the door. Tony is a big man with plenty of belly and he lost his accent twenty years ago, but he hates to forget it.

"Two go in—only one comes out," he said.

"The one that's still in," I said, "has to stay till I get back."

"O. K., Mac," he said. "If the police come?"

"Have the police ever come?"

"Not yet."

"Then relax."

Tony said some words in Italian. I knew he would be all right. I had done him some favors. I went out and Larry followed me into the car.

"The last job of baby-sitting I did," he said, "I got five bucks an hour."

I got the car going and raced it down the street to the turn toward the hospital that loomed, high and bleak, two blocks away.

"Did the kid say anything?" I asked him.

140

"Only that he was willing to shoot himself."

"Did you give him the chance?"

"Mac."

"I'm sorry."

He didn't say any more and I parked in a red zone in front of the hospital and we went inside. It was quiet in there and I got the stiff treatment from the lady at the receiving desk. I asked her about a blonde lady and a cop named Donovan.

"Lieutenant Donovan is on the fourth floor," she said.

I headed for the elevator. She called after me, "Wait! You can't go up there now—"

Larry was beside me as the elevator door opened and we stepped in together. It was dual-controlled, now switched to automatic. I pushed the fourth floor button and tried not to chew my nails.

"Had anything to eat lately?" I asked him.

"Practically nothing else," he said.

"I may ask you to stay here a while."

"You're the boss."

The fourth floor corridor was dim and quiet. Halfway along toward the rear of the building was a large alcove, lamp lit. It would be the nurses' station and waiting room. I saw the shadows of three men seated on a sofa against the wall, but they were around the corner and I couldn't tell who they were. Larry and I went down that way.

A nurse sat at a small desk slanting across the alcove and facing the corridor. The sofa was against the near wall. The three men were Donovan and two cops I didn't know. When Larry and I reached the corner of the alcove, Donovan rose ponderously.

"You called me?" I said to him.

He put an arm across my shoulders and led me into the corridor. I went along because I had to know.

"She's in room four-fourteen, son," he said. "If I was you, I wouldn't see her now."

"You're not me."

"I know."

I pulled away from him, looking for the room numbers over the doors. He came after me.

"Somebody called in and told us where she was—in some alley."

"All right."

He stayed on my heels as I went along the corridor.

"So the boys picked her up. Whoever it was called, some guy, said she should be brought here and the bills would be taken care of."

Impatient, I turned on him.

"O. K.," I said. "So you brought her in and the bills will be paid. I could have told you that. Why are you hanging around here? Sorelle did it to her. I told you that. There's an eyewitness—in a room on Ontario Street. You tired or something, you got to hang around a hospital? Couldn't you at least send somebody to tuck Sorelle in bed?"

"She won't make a complaint about Sorelle. She keeps saying, 'Forget about it. Leave me alone.'"

"Then I make the complaint; now, officially."

His face was impassive.

"We've got other business too, Mac. With this girl. I'll want to talk to her. I'll have to leave the boys here—"

"Those potbellied geniuses?"

For a moment he was no longer impassive. He looked at me with the resignation of a desperate father.

"All right, shamus," he said, "I guess nobody can help you."

He turned away. My teeth worked on my lip. I had got him sore and let him walk away once tonight and I had got in trouble. Maybe it was time to quit making the mistakes.

"Donovan," I said softly.

He turned back.

"I'm sorry," I said. "Hang around. But my man stays too."

"Larry?"

I nodded.

"That's up to you, son," he said.

He went on back to the alcove then and I went down the corridor to Room 414. The door opened as I got there and a man in a white jacket came out, followed by a nurse.

"Is she in there?" I asked.

"Yes," the nurse said, "but I don't think—"

I started to push past her, then turned back. The guy in the jacket was walking away toward the alcove.

"He's a doctor?" I said.

"An interne," the nurse said.

I went back to the alcove and motioned to Larry, who got up. The interne was leaning over the nurse's desk. I touched his arm and he turned to look at me.

"This is the doctor," I said to Larry. "He's the only one you'll let into her room."

Larry nodded. The doctor looked at the nurse.

"Who is this?" he said and the nurse shrugged.

I didn't have time to explain. Maybe Donovan would explain. I went back to the corridor and the nurse had disappeared. I went to the door of her room and took hold of the knob. It turned quietly in my hand and the door opened easily. Inside the room it was dark except for a faint night, light beside the bed. There was a small mound under the bedclothes, but I couldn't see her face. I pushed the door shut and it clicked slightly. Her voice came distantly from the bed.

"Who is it?"

"Mac," I said.

I heard the rustle of the sheet and saw the white of it move upward and her white hands. When I got to the bed she had pulled the sheet over her face. I took hold of it, but she clamped down on it with her hands and spoke through it.

"No, Mac. Not now."

There was a chair beside the bed and I sat down in it. I put my hand on one of hers and she relaxed it, but she wouldn't take hold of mine.

"He did it because I hit him," I said after while. "And because he found out you were with me."

"No, Mac."

"But I didn't know about you when I hit him."

"Please—" The dark was swimming around me. There were strange shapes in it.

"That's why you would leave the hotel. He was your brother. You would trust him."

She didn't say anything.

"All your life, you did whatever he told you to do," I said. "It was Barney who closed out the dress business, wasn't it?"

She didn't say anything.

"Did you really want to close down? go away? leave your apartment to that—"

"Mac, do the police still think it was Norman who killed her?"

"No," I said. "Not any more."

"Then can't you forget it now—the case—just let everything go?"

"Forgive me, baby," I said, "don't ask for promises. I made a lot of mistakes. I'll try not to make any more. But don't ask me—"

"All my life, Mac, I though Barney was being good to me. He gave me money, protected me. He sent me to school. He set me up in business. I never knew that he was just doing it for himself—sometimes for his conscience, sometimes for profit."

"Easy, honey…"

"But now I know—in all my life, there were only two people who were really good to me. Aaron Krupp—and you."

Her hand moved, then closed on mine.

"Did the doctor give you a shot?" I asked.

"Yes."

"Then you should sleep now."

Her voice was far-off now and I could barely hear it. But I heard it all right.

"Kiss me, Mac."

I stood up and reached for the sheet again, but she held it tightly.

"No, please. Through the sheet, Mac."

I found her mouth with my fingers and leaned over her. There were the odors of gauze and medication, of freshly laundered linen, and through it all, faintly but still there, the lingering, fading fragrance of gardenia, still hers, still part of her.

I kissed her mouth through the sheet and it was warm and trembling against mine.

"So long, baby," I said. "I'll be back."

She didn't answer and I walked out of the room and down the corridor quietly.

CHAPTER 30

Only the old late standbys were left at Tony's when I got back; three or four of them, slumped here and there over a bar or booth table. Tony was at the cash register, counting. He gave me a big Italian gesture with the hands in the air.

"Such a noise he made. Mac, will you bring another type the next time?"

"Wanted out, did he?"

"Wanted out? Wanted a lawyer, wanted the cops—everything!"

One of the customers raised his head from the bar and looked at me blearily. He was a dead-beat lush who had once been a promising attorney.

"I was almost persuaded," he said, "to take his case. It sounded like he had one."

He shook his head sadly.

"I thought it over," he said, "and I guess not. It might interfere with my other career."

He put his head down again on the bar.

I went to the door of the back room and it was locked. When I looked around, Tony was taking a big ring of keys down off the wall. He threw them to me and I missed the catch. I picked them up.

There was a telephone booth in the corner near the back room door and I went into it and dialed Aaron Krupp. He answered after the first ring. I guess he'd been sitting there beside the phone all night.

"It's Mac," I said, "and I'm with Norman at a place across the street from my office. I think it would be all right for him to go home now. I don't think Donovan will call again."

"Shall I drive over and get him?"

"That was what I hoped you would say."

"In half an hour, Mac."

I hung up and opened the door to the back room. After standing there a minute, I walked through to the outside wall and opened a window. The air that came in across Tony's garbage cans smelled pretty good. I went back and closed the door and switched on the light. It wasn't a bright light and I knew it wouldn't hurt his eyes.

Norman Krupp lay on his back on a folding army cot at one side of the room. The part of his face that I could see looked pale. He had thrown his arm over his eyes when I turned on the light. I saw his lips move but I didn't hear any sound. I sat down on a chair against the far wall between two stacks of empty beer cases. After a while he took his arm away from his eyes and looked at me. When he saw who it was, he turned again and looked at the wall.

"Can you tell me about the pictures now?" I said.

I waited a long time and decided he wasn't going to talk. I had opened my mouth to ask him something else when his voice came, distantly, as he spoke into the wall.

"It was that crazy Peterson. She had made some kind of contract to model for him, illustrations for those pamphlets of his. I did it with her, just as a gag. They were pretty corny, all about the *Wages of Sin,* you know?"

"I guess maybe I know."

"There wasn't anything wrong with them. They weren't dirty pictures."

"O. K. Why did the girl—Diana—why did she go in for this?"

He flared up. Weakly, but he flared, like a nearly spent candle.

"She didn't *go in* for it. She just did it. She had this contract with Peterson."

"Couldn't she have broken the contract?"

"She thought she ought to help him. Even if he wasn't really her father, she felt guilty; he had helped her when she needed it. He was almost like a father to her. I don't know—she would have felt guilty!"

"I had a father once," I said. "I never felt guilty about him. He got drunk one night and walked in front of a truck. He was a sick man and I didn't know it then, but I didn't feel guilty about it—not then or ever."

"You're different!"

"Excuse me," I said. "I didn't meant to argue. Go ahead."

"I guess she was afraid of him too. He was kind of mean—"

"In what way?"

"I'm not sure. Sometimes it seemed as if he were holding something over her head."

"Or maybe," I said, "it was Barney Sorelle she was afraid of."

His head jerked a little and his eyes traveled over my face, then looked away.

Easy, Mac, I thought. Don't put words in his mouth. Only for God's sake, let it come out right. Let it come out the way I want to hear it.

"I only saw Barney Sorelle once," Norman said. "At that nightclub, the House of Jazz. He owns it."

146

"And a warehouse on the West Side, next door to a photographer's studio?"

"I don't know."

"Are you afraid of Barney Sorelle too?" I asked.

"Me?" he said, flaring again. "Certainly not. Why would I be afraid of him?"

"He's what they call a tough cookie; a wronggo; a baddy; a racketeer; a crook—"

"I wouldn't know," he said. "Live and let live."

I had been sitting with the chair tipped back against the wall. Now I eased it down slowly, got up and headed for the door. Then I turned back and looked at his white face against the soiled, brown cot.

"What did you do with the forty-five hundred bucks you drew out of your savings account the other day?" I asked.

The cot squeaked as he jumped. He even raised himself to one elbow to look at me.

"How did you know about that?"

"The cops told me about it. Donovan checked it. What did you do with it?"

He stared at me for a long time and then he dropped his head back onto the cot.

"I gave it to somebody," he said.

"To whom?"

"To Ben Champlain."

"The photographer?"

"I guess you know him too."

"Not well. Why did you give it to him?"

"He came to me, with some of the pictures, of Marta and me—"

"Don't call her Marta!"

I was shocked at the sound of my own voice. He stared at me.

"Go ahead," I said. "What about the pictures?"

"He told me Mart—she was going to get in trouble over them and he needed money to fix the cops."

"You believed this?"

"I didn't care about him, but I was afraid for her."

"And a little for yourself?"

"I didn't have anything to be afraid of."

"So you gave him the money."

"It was my own money. I didn't have to steal it."

"Do you suppose he kept it all for himself?"

"What do you mean?"

I thought it over. He was sick now. This was no time to give him the whole picture. He'd get the rest of it soon enough.

"Nothing," I said. "Let it go."

Suddenly I felt tired. There were white spots flickering in the air wherever I looked. I blinked and rubbed a hand over my eyes to shut them out. I started out the door, then turned back once more and went to stand near the cot.

"Norman," I said, "I guess I was a little rough on you. You're all right and I hope you have a long, happy life. We live on opposite sides of the street. You do fine on your own side, but when you get over on my side, you're likely to run into trouble. Likewise with me. It's nice out on that campus, but I wouldn't know how to handle myself out there. That's for you."

He was looking at me differently now from any way he had looked before. He was looking at me man to man—his kind of man to my kind—and it felt good. I managed to work up a grin.

"There'll be a lot of stuff in the papers tomorrow," I said, "and you won't like some of it. But you're too solid to let it throw you. Some time, if you want to, come around and talk to me about it. Maybe I can help. There won't be any charge…O. K.?"

He managed to grin back, slowly at first, then a little bigger and straight out.

"O. K., Mac," he said.

"You want to use Tony's washroom before your old man—your father gets here?"

"Yeah," he said, struggling to his feet.

I opened the door and waited while he went through it. I showed him the way to the washroom and he turned in that direction. He had gone a few feet when he looked back and smiled again.

"Thanks, Mac," he said.

I waved at him and sat down at Tony's bar. He brought me a brandy with water on the side.

CHAPTER 31

I went into the phone booth and dialed the House of Jazz. A man answered and I asked for Mr. Sorelle. He said Sorelle wasn't there and I asked where I could reach him. He said maybe at home. He didn't know the number.

I called Samuel in Donovan's office.

"I need Barney Sorelle's private, unlisted, residence phone number," I said.

"It may take a little time," Samuel said.

"I'll wait," I said.

It was stuffy standing in the booth and I walked around the place while Tony swept the floor with a long push broom, and finally the phone rang. It was Samuel and he gave me the number.

"You boys all over your mad?" I asked.

"Let's say there's been called a truce."

"How long have I got?"

"How long do you need?"

"Thirty or forty years," I said.

"You should—"

"Live so long," I said and hung up.

Life was getting awfully full of trite phrases. I dialed the number Samuel had given me and pretty soon the phone went up and a cold voice asked who was calling. I told him and asked for Mr. Sorelle. He went away and I held the phone some more. The next voice I heard was that of Mr. Sorelle himself, in person.

"The smart shamus," he said.

"I thought you would be interested to know," I said, "that your boy Champlain has been knocking down on you."

"I didn't hear that, bright boy."

"Champlain," I said, "and you hear good. He blackmailed Norman Krupp and got forty-five hundred bucks out of him. I don't know how much of it he gave you. He gave some of it to a girl who is now dead."

"Who?"

I took a deep breath.

"Sorelle," I said, "do the faces of your dead slaves ever visit you in the night? I gave you a tip. You might want to talk to Champlain, before I get around to it. The last time I saw him, he was hard at work in his studio, taking pictures of the gadget you dropped beside the body of Diana Peterson."

I hung up and stepped out of the booth. Norman had come back from the washroom and he looked a little better. We sat down in a booth and I had a couple of brandies, while we waited for Aaron Krupp. When he came, Norman spoke to him somewhat sheepishly and went out to the car. I walked to the door with Mr. Krupp. We shook hands.

"Marta Sandor," I said, "is in the hospital. I know it's late. But after you take Norman home, I think it would be a shot in the arm for her if you would go to see her."

His big face was grim.

"Is she in pain?" he said.

"Considerable," I said.

"I'll go," he said. "Thank you, Mac, for me and the boy. You will figure out a bill and send it—"

"I'll figure out a bill. Goodnight."

He went out and I watched while he got in the car and drove away. Tony was waiting to lock his front door. It was three-forty-five in the a.m. and he had had a long day. That I should have such a day—

"One more brandy," I said.

Tony shook his jowls.

"No more brandies. Bad for the stomach."

I went around behind the bar and found the bottle. I poured myself a generous shot and stood there, drinking it, while Tony glared at me across the bar.

"Mac," he said, "you are going to fall apart inside, in little pieces—"

"I think so," I said, dunking the glass in the washing fluid. "But not for the reasons you are thinking."

I headed for the door.

"You go to bed now?" Tony said, following me.

"Later," I said. "Goodnight, friend."

He was mumbling to himself as he opened the door to let me out, then pushed it shut again behind me.

I had left my car across the street and I walked toward it slowly, inhaling deeply as I went. The inhaling didn't help my lungs, but it closed my mind for a few seconds. There was a guy walking slowly on the sidewalk in front of the office and I stopped a few feet from the car and waited for his face to show under the streetlight. But he had heard me and turned back to approach the car.

"Mac," he said. It was the voice of George Keeler.

I opened the door on the driver's side and climbed in. George opened the other door and got in beside me.

"It's late," I said.

"Mac," he said, "I just came from Peterson. He's out of his head. I think the boys in white will come for him any minute."

"You don't say."

"I found out something that maybe you ought to know."

I rested my head against the steering wheel and waited.

"About a year and a half ago," George said, "a girl named Diana Petersen was picked up on a D and D. She had no previous record and she got probation and was released in custody of her father, a Carl Peterson. Peterson was in court, with a birth certificate."

"Whose?"

"The girl's. But the certificate was phony. It was a photostat and it had been faked on a counterfeit form."

"All right."

"So there's proof Peterson wasn't the dead girl's real father."

"So."

"So what I want to know," he said, "is who is Marta Sandor?"

My hands on the wheel were clammy.

"There were maybe three guys who really knew who Marta Sandor was," I said, "and one of them is dead."

"Mac, be a good guy—"

"George, will you go home or something?"

"You're not very friendly tonight."

"I like you fine," I said. "I love you, boy. But I've got work to do."

He climbed out of the car.

"Will you do this, Mac—?"

"I will. As soon as it's cleaned up. I'll give you a ring. I'll see you're the first to know."

He closed the door without slamming it and leaned on it. His manner had changed. He was no longer pushing for information.

"Good luck, Mac," he said.

"Thanks, George. I'll call you."

He stepped back and I started the car and drove to Michigan, where I turned north. The wind against my face was damp and cold.

CHAPTER 32

The parking area behind Ben Champlain's studio was dark this time, with no light coming through the rear windows. A Cadillac sedan was parked carelessly askew across two of the spaces. There was another, older-model sedan nearby. The heavy steel door of the lab was closed and no doubt locked.

I had walked down the alley from the deserted street after parking my car around the corner out of sight. No one had challenged me and I had heard no footsteps but my own. I put my ear against the steel door, but I couldn't hear anything going on inside. I tried the knob, but the door was locked. So there was the problem of getting somebody on the inside to open it for me.

The old sedan was nearest to the door. The key was in the ignition and I climbed in and started the motor. I let it warm up briefly, then gunned it toward the wall. It made a good big crash hitting the wall and I had climbed out and got myself flat beside the door before the echo died away.

Light came on over my left shoulder and I had the gun out, as once before, when footsteps sounded and the door lock grated. A long rectangle of light grew on the pavement, a big man's shadow nearly filling it, I held my breath, waiting, and the shadow advanced slowly, the head disappearing, the body widening grotesquely as the light angle lengthened. I couldn't tell whether it was Bronk or the other one, but it didn't matter much.

He came on through the door and stopped, standing on the pavement. After a minute, he turned toward the wall where I had crashed the sedan. He had gone half a dozen steps when I got into the lighted frame of the door and hissed at him. He spun around, saw me with the gun and stood still. I beckoned to him and he came slowly toward me. When he got into the light, I saw it was Bronk.

His mind was very slow indeed. First he had to establish the recognition. Then he had to figure out something to do about it. What he figured on I'm not sure, but he opened his mouth. I don't know whether he meant to yell a warning or to say "hello," but I didn't wait to find out. I smashed his mouth with the back of my hand and he stepped back and felt quickly to see whether there was any blood. I spoke to him *sotto voce.*

"Come inside, slow," I said.

I backed into the lab, trusting nobody had come to check on Bronk and he came along warily now, his dull eyes puzzled. I motioned to him to close the door easily, and he did it, but it didn't latch.

So the hell with it, I thought.

I backed against one of the assembly tables. There was nothing behind me but pictures piled in neat stacks. All nudes. Bronk stood there staring at me.

"Where are they?" I asked, whispering.

He didn't answer. I couldn't expect him to answer. It would take a while for the message to get to his brain and back to where he could handle it.

Then I heard the voices—Sorelle's big one mainly—coming from some place not far off. I listened briefly. He was throwing quite a tantrum.

"…make me get up in the middle of the night and come down here—you think this lousy mail-order deal is a big thing with me? Peanuts! Pin money!…"

Another voice mumbled something and Sorelle's cut across it.

"And you had to try to hold out. That's what kills me. A chiseler—knocking down on the side. Trying to tie me into a stinking blackmail rap. The shamus is out to get me and you know it." His voice hardened a little. "Maybe you'd like to see him do it. Guys have drowned in that lake out there for less."

The other voice came in again, pleadingly this time, and again Sorelle interrupted.

"Shut up! I got to take care of you and I got to take care of the shamus. Maybe I can figure out a way you can take care of each other."

More mumbling and then Sorelle's voice, quieter now.

"I guess that's the only out for you. You get rid of the shamus and I'll forget the whole deal. You like that suggestion? Simple. All you got to do —sneak up on him some dark night—like tonight—and hit him in the head. You'll have that fat cop, Donovan, after you for the rest of your life, but maybe you can figure a way around that too. O. K., Champlain?"

No mumbling now. Only silence. I straightened away from the table, motioning to Bronk.

He started to shake his head and I made a pass at him with the gun. He turned then and walked through the lab into the corridor that led to the front of the building. I followed about six paces behind him. Once he stopped and looked back and I nudged him forward.

"I'll do all the talking," I said. "You just walk in as if nothing had happened. You heard what Sorelle said. I've got nothing to lose by pulling this trigger."

Ahead of us, the double door stood ajar. Light spilled out of the warehouse onto the floor. Fortunately, the door opened outward into the corridor and would screen me until I was well inside.

Bronk paused, just short of the door and I had to nudge him again. He went on then, around the door into the light and again I was in the warehouse with the overhead crane, the ropes and pulleys, the deep shadows everywhere except in the brightly lighted area near the door where the long mail-ting tables were lined up.

Sorelle was pacing back and forth the length of the alley between the tables. When we stepped into the light he had just completed one trip to the far end, had turned and was heading back in our direction. I stepped out from behind Bronk.

"Don't let me interrupt your conversation," I said.

Sorelle stopped abruptly with his squat body leaning forward, one foot in front of the other. His fat hands moved restlessly, his fingers twitching. I saw that there were two others in the room: Ben Champlain, still in his shirtsleeves, stood on my left beside one of the tables; Bronk's partner, Alex, was on the other side near Sorelle.

I watched Sorelle fight to find his voice, but he was too full of rage and frustration. He stood a moment longer, poised unsteadily in that forward-leaning stance, and then he started for me, both hands up in front of him, grabbing at me before he was within any kind of reach. I told him to stop and he kept coming. I shot onto the floor in front of him and white dust swirled up around his ankles. He stopped.

"We don't have to have trouble," I said, "unless you want to make it."

He finally managed to say something.

"How are you coming with your big frame-up, bright boy?" he said. "Find any pieces missing?"

"Only one," I said. "I don't know why you had to kill Howard Jones."

Bronk took a step forward and I waved him back with the gun.

"He was an old man," he mumbled thickly. "I only hit him a couple of times—huh, Alex?"

"Shut up!" Sorelle said.

The atmosphere was full of talk and I didn't feel healthy. I had a hunch that both Sorelle and Alex across from Champlain were equipped to shoot, and it required too much vigilance to watch them and listen to Sorelle at the same time. If Sorelle should come any farther forward, he would cut Alex out of my vision for just long enough. They were all on edge and a little scared and they'd probably shoot me just to ease the ten-

154

sion. Meanwhile, I had plenty of tension myself. I couldn't disarm them personally, because it would mean going too close to them. I was more or less frozen in position and all I had to work with was my tongue. I didn't feel sharp enough to take advantage of it. Still, I had to try.

"I can't figure out," I said, talking directly to Sorelle, "why Champlain faked that photo I found, the one that showed Diana Peterson on the sofa with Norman Krupp, only with your sister's head pasted over Diana's. Why was your sister in it?"

Sorelle turned very slowly to look at Champlain, who stood stiff and silent against the long table. When he spoke his voice was hoarse and low-pitched.

"Well, Champlain—tell me about it."

Champlain chose not to speak.

"Was that another blackmail deal? Did you figure on working it with me—with Barney Sorelle?"

I was sorry I'd started it. He was dangerously close to flipping his fat lid and that would put me in a bad corner. I would have to calm him down again.

"Take it easy," I said, "you're all stewing in the same pot. Everybody's double-crossed everybody else. You had your boys beat up your own sister, because you were afraid she'd spill something to me. She couldn't, of course, because she didn't really know enough. Peterson tried to make a grandstand play by going to the papers. Big, free publicity deal. I don't know how you disciplined him. Maybe you haven't got around to it. Then you tried to screw everything up by coming to me—to hire me. The hidden ball play. Obscure the issues, throw everybody off.

"But you couldn't buy, could you, Sorelle? Tell me something, what would you like to buy right now, this minute, if you had the price?"

Sorelle drew a long, shuddering breath and let his shoulders slump forward. He looked at me out of half-closed eyes, so that he seemed to be peering upward.

"All right, shamus," he said quietly enough. "What's the play? What did you come for?"

"Maybe," I said, "we can make a deal."

"You're doing the talking."

"You write out a confession to the murder of Diana Peterson and I'll forget the mail-order business and the blackmail against Norman Krupp."

He just stared at me. I reached with my left hand for the fountain pen in my coat pocket and tossed it at him. It fell on the floor at his feet and he made no move to pick it up.

Faintly and far off, through the walls of the building. I heard a car motor. I didn't bother to figure it out. I just tried to wrap things up and get some relief from the tension that was building in me like a self-winding spring. It was nearly at the snapping point and I didn't want to go on with it. I wanted to walk away and lie down somewhere and let my breath run out.

"The trouble with guys like you," I said to Sorelle, "—you get scared. You haven't really got the guts to stand up. The mail-order business in the smut market is small money, but it would be embarrassing to have to explain it.

"Diana Peterson was a nobody. Who would miss her? You got scared about her—maybe she would talk. I don't know how you managed to get her on the floor without any clothes on. Maybe she agreed to make one more picture for auld lang syne. Anyway you set the scene, and then you set the pillow over her head and held it there till she quit fighting."

Sorelle's eyes were wide and fascinated as he watched me, listening. When I quit talking he shook his head slowly from side to side.

"You are crazy," he said. "That's not true."

I shrugged.

"Who cares?" I said. Something was swimming around in front of my eyes. Maybe it was the room. I had nausea. "Who cares whether it's true? I can prove it. I've got the evidence. The silver chain that you left there… Got your name on it, Sorelle—"

His face blurred before my eyes. Bronk was still standing where he had stopped when we first came in, five feet ahead of me, to my left, turned to face Sorelle. I guess his mind had been working overtime and had come up with something. Anyway, in the instant of my blurred vision he swung around without warning and before I could move or shoot or even shout anything, he had ploughed into my midsection with his shoulder and I heard my gun clatter away over the cement floor. Then I didn't hear any more, because the combination of the blow in my stomach and the banging of my head on the floor knocked me far, far out.

CHAPTER 33

I couldn't have been out for long, because when I opened my eyes I saw that Sorelle was in the same position as when I had still held the gun. Myself, I was no longer in the same position. I was standing by one of the tables with Bronk on one side of me and Alex on the other. They had pulled my arms up behind me and I couldn't have taken a step without breaking one or both of them. My head was pounding dully and my vision wasn't clear. Still, I could make out Sorelle's flushed, enraged face.

As I watched, he approached me slowly, stopping a couple of feet away. His heavy lips formed words, but I couldn't make them out. It occurred to me that he was cursing, maybe in another language. Pretty soon he quit it and when he spoke again the words were clear enough.

"So I guess it comes down to this, shamus. Either you or me, and I think now it will be you. You got any last minute messages for anybody?"

"Only one," I said. "For your sister."

He lifted his hand and slammed the back of it into my face. The big ring cut into my flesh and I felt the earlier wound swell and dampen. I let my head stay where it had fallen, so he hit me again to straighten me up. I pulled some against my arms but they were rigid and almost numb. I saw that Ben Champlain had come to look at me over Sorelle's shoulder. Sorelle turned to him quickly.

"He's yours, Champlain. Remember the deal?"

"I remember."

"You got any ideas?"

"Sure, Barney. Leave it to me."

"Leave it to you… I don't know."

Champlain stabbed a thumb back over his shoulder.

"The catwalk is forty feet from the floor," he said. "A guy could fall off that and split his head open and it would be an industrial accident, wouldn't it?"

Sorelle gazed at him for a long time, then nodded slowly. "I guess maybe it would," he said.

"I guess I didn't give you enough credit."

He turned back to me.

"You want to climb up there and fall off, shamus?" he said. "To oblige the boys?"

He was giving it all he had. I guess he had read the literature about Al Capone and was testing his own theatrical instinct. I couldn't deny that he had me where he wanted me. The old-fashioned methods were still effective. Only it would be nice if I could get to him just for a moment.

"Maybe we could both go," I said.

"Yeah," he said. "Hand in hand. Hold out your hand, bright boy."

I didn't bother to try.

"What's the matter, you can't hold out your hand? You tired or something?"

I was fed up with the game. I was fed up with everything that had to do with the death of Diana Peterson. It looked to me as if they had me ready for the feast and how could it matter now? I could get in one more good lick and maybe he would remember.

He was close enough to me and he was in the correct position, leaning forward a little, peering at me. I decided he was nearsighted. I would have laughed then, if my throat hadn't been aching.

Hell, I thought, he couldn't have read the inscription on the silver pin anyway.

I lifted my foot, fast and hard and kicked him, low, where it would hurt. I felt something give in him under the impact. I saw him sit down backwards on the floor, staring up at me in some surprise. Then I looked away.

I don't remember much of the next few minutes. Sorelle worked on me for a while, then I guess it was Bronk, but I never knew for sure. By then I couldn't feel much. I couldn't feel it when they wrapped the rope around my chest and arms, pinning them to my sides, and around my ankles. I couldn't hear anything except a distant roaring. So I have no memory of that time either.

Memory picks up at a fantastic point, when I found myself dangling from the end of a giant hook, rising slowly toward the ceiling. By the time my head reached the level of the catwalk floor, I got back enough vision to see there was somebody standing on it, leaning over the railing, ready to pull me in. I remember glancing down into the yellow patch of light on the floor and seeing Sorelle and Bronk gaping up at me. I remember spitting toward them and missing.

Then they were hauling me in over the rail of the catwalk and detaching the hook from the ropes around my chest. They were Alex and Champlain. They worked quickly, got the hook free and let it swing out again over the rail. I guessed there must be a counterweight at the bottom to hold the tackle up in position. They didn't speak to each other, nor to me, until Alex said quietly, "Take the ropes off now?"

And Champlain said, "No. Afterward."

I ached everywhere I had a nerve. My head was the size of a bushel basket and there were shooting pains in my stomach and chest. I glanced down over the rail of the catwalk and knew I wouldn't hurt much longer. It was a long, long way to the cold, hard floor. If I could be lucky enough to land on my head, I'd hardly notice it. I kept blinking my eyes, trying to keep Sorelle in focus. He kept shifting into and out of my vision—or maybe it was my vision that kept going off and coming back on, like a blinking neon sign, but irregularly.

Champlain pushed me hastily toward the rail. He pushed too hard and I couldn't keep my balance because of my bound ankles. I fell against the rail and toppled to the floor, Champlain cursed and the two of them pulled me to my feet again. I leaned against the rail, looking down, and it was a good place to be because I was very sick in the stomach.

I was looking for Sorelle again, finding him, losing him and finding him once more, when a wide shadow grew beyond him in the open doorway. I think I knew who it was right away, the way you sometimes know you're dreaming, even while you're still asleep. But it didn't register in my head till I heard that gruff, disgruntled voice, sweeter than any Irish tenor, saying.

"Break it up and stand still."

And I knew it was Donovan and that there were four cops coming in with him. I felt Champlain and Alex freeze beside me. Below, Sorelle and Bronk had whirled at the sound of the voice and now they stood with their hands in the air, looking into Donovan's gun. His four boys flanked him on both sides. He looked up at the catwalk.

"Come on down, the two of you," he said.

Alex turned and started back toward the near corner, where there must have been a ladder. But Champlain, twisting suddenly, broke in the other direction and ran, bent double, along the catwalk toward the far end of the building. Two guns barked down below and I saw Champlain, just as he reached the shadowed corner, lurch against the rail on his face. I looked back toward Donovan.

"Can you get down from there?" he said.

My lips were thick and bruised and it hurt to talk.

"Not right now," I said. "I can wait."

Donovan jerked his head at one of the cops.

"Go up there and cut loose the crazy shamus," he said.

Alex walked into the light with his hands up and one of the cops moved quickly past him toward the ladder in the corner. After a minute his head appeared at the top of the ladder and then he was walking toward me, digging a knife from his pocket as he came.

"Hi, Mac," he said. "How'd you get in a shape like this?"

"I ran into a door," I said.

He began sawing on the ropes and finally my arms were free. But I was impatient and I asked him for the knife and sat down to cut the ropes from my ankles.

"You better get back and help Donovan," I said.

He went away. I got the ropes off, grabbed the railing and pulled myself up, but my feet had gone to sleep and I went down on my knees right away.

Down below, they had turned the three playmates around. The boys were putting handcuffs on Bronk and Alex, but Sorelle still had his hands up by his shoulders, waiting.

I started to pull myself up again, using the rail for support, when I saw Champlain rising painfully on the catwalk up ahead. I reached for my gun and found I no longer had one. I started after him, holding to the rail, while the blood rushed back into my feet like the stabbing of a million needles.

Champlain floundered toward the wall and his hand went up, groping. I saw him yank down hard on some kind of a handle and the light went out. Feet pounded suddenly on the floor below and Donovan's voice rose harshly.

"Hold it, Sorelle!"

But the feet went on pounding and Donovan yelled for a light. Somebody finally got one on, a thin flashlight beam, and there was some shooting, but I didn't hear anybody yell.

There could be only one direction in which Sorelle could run and I moved along the catwalk, looking down, trying to chart his course. I couldn't hear his footsteps any more over the confusion of sound the cops made, but I heard a faint rattle and squeaking at the far end of the warehouse and then saw the thin gray light of the street through a partly open door and heard the sound the door made closing.

I ran along the catwalk and my feet were all right now. I bumped into Champlain, leaning against the rail and he put a hand on me weakly. I shook it off and went on with a hand out in front to find my way. It brushed against the steel rungs of a ladder and I went down fast, gripping the rungs with my hands and letting my feet slide over them to save time. Near the bottom I missed with one hand, lost my grip and fell the last eight feet to the floor. I got up and felt my way along the wall till I found the door. It hadn't latched when Sorelle left it and when I touched it with my hand it swung open, letting me outside into a narrow alley.

CHAPTER 34

He was fat and probably short-winded and he couldn't have got far. If he had any sense left, he would first go around back and try to get in his car.

The alley was paved and dark, with the brick wall of the warehouse on one side and a high wire fence on the other. It was a distance of fifty yards from the door through which I had come to the rear of the building and I ran all the way, stopping short of the corner to catch my breath before going on around to the parking area.

Straight ahead, across the wide space between the back of Sorelle's warehouse and the back of another that faced on the next street, was a long loading platform with a couple of trucks pulled up beside it. I had stepped into the open and started to my left toward the parking area behind the studio when I saw movement on the platform across the way. He had come out from behind the far truck and was moving slowly, close to the wall of the building. Farther along, to my right, there were more trucks.

I ran quietly across the open space to the front end of the truck and crouched behind the wheel on the alley side. I saw him for a moment, twenty feet ahead of me, as he passed a door with a frosted glass panel. Then I lost him against the black of the building wall.

The next truck was forty feet ahead, not far from the cross street that would put him in the clear. I waited till he had nearly reached it, then sprinted for the truck. I ducked down again and tried to find him over the hood. But I couldn't see him and I couldn't hear him move.

A motor purred and headlights swung into the street beyond the loading area. I stood up behind the hood of the truck and in the moment's beam of the passing lights I saw Sorelle on the platform, standing above me with a gun in his hand.

I dropped behind the hood and heard him empty the gun. I could hear the slugs crashing into the metal of the hood. There was a crash of glass and I guessed he had thrown the gun. His footsteps pounded then and I ran out from behind the truck and scrambled onto the platform behind him.

There were some black trash barrels on the platform and Sorelle crashed into them, falling and rolling toward the edge. I caught up with him then and helped him over with my foot. When I jumped down beside him, he came up at me slugging.

I guess he had learned to fight in the slum he came from and he was tough and dirty. But I had learned it in another slum and we were evenly matched. My ribs ached and he got to them several times, but he was breathing in gasps and his timing was off. I stumbled once and fell backwards and he came down on me like a cat. We rolled over and over then till we came up against the platform and I pushed up, dragging him with me. There was no force in his blows any more and I knew he was ready to quit. But I was only getting started. I pounded him back along the platform and he fell on his knees. I jerked him back up again, Dent him back over the rough wood and began to pound him in the face, yelling at him all the time. I didn't know what I was yelling till Donovan told me later. I was beating him and screaming at the top of my voice, "Not for her—not for Diana—you stupid, outmoded son of a bitch! For him! For Howie Jones…!"

Then Donovan was pulling me off him. I started to fight Donovan and he had to slap me once to make me quit. Then I sat down on the ground with my head between my knees and learned again how to breathe. I heard cops moving around and voices and they faded and pretty soon Donovan was there alone with me, his hand on my shoulder.

"Come on, Mac," he said. "I'll take you home."

I got on my feet and Donovan grabbed me to steady me.

"No," I said. "I've got one more call to make."

"Don't make it, son," he said.

"I have to."

There was some silence and then he said, "You want to pick up your own car?"

"That would be fine," I said.

He walked with me through the alley out to the street and helped me into the car. After he went away I sat for quite a while and then I started it up. I couldn't see very well, but I could see all right to drive. I knew the route now.

* * * *

The hospital corridor was dim and warm, as before, and very quiet. In a few minutes it would be five o'clock and the shifts would change and people would begin to wake up. But now it had that complete hush that falls in the last hour of sleep. I had a little trouble at the desk downstairs and the nurse on the fourth floor frowned at me when I passed the alcove where Larry Evans still sat, waiting to be relieved. I nodded to him and he lay down on the sofa. There was a cop there, sitting in a chair.

I went to the door of Room 414 and went in. The night light was still on and I sat down in the chair beside the bed and closed my eyes for a while. She seemed to be asleep and her face had been turned away from the door so all I saw was her blonde hair spread out on the pillow. But when I opened my eyes again she had turned her head toward me. I saw that there were bandages on her face, but in the dim light I couldn't see them clearly, nor anything about her face that was familiar. I guessed that she was still asleep, because if she had wakened and found me there, she would have covered her face with the sheet.

I was aware that Aaron Krupp was in the room too, but it seemed natural for him to be there and neither of us had spoken to the other. He was sitting in a high-backed chair on the other side of the bed and I could see his big hands on the arms of the chair and his big face, pale in the half dark.

I had to talk it out. I knew I had to talk, and yet when I did, it sounded like another voice, not mine. The words kept sticking in my throat.

"Marta Sandor—what was your real name, honey? Molly Sorelle, maybe. Or Catherine. Or Martha. It doesn't make and difference. Marta is a nice name. I like it fine.

"Diana Peterson liked it too, didn't she? The way she liked your clothes, your apartment, the way you lived. And she took it, didn't she? She took it all and used it her way. 'She wanted to be me,' you said. And finally she was. She stole everything, your whole identity. Everything that was you."

I stopped and the sound of her breathing had changed, but I couldn't look at her eyes.

"And you had to let her do it, because Barney wanted it that way and all your life you did what Barney told you to do. Whenever he gave you something—like the dress business—he took it away again."

Without conscious effort I looked at the big shape of Aaron Krupp in the chair across from me. He hadn't moved.

"You might have let it all go, if she hadn't turned on your friend, too. Was that when it happened, inside you? Was that when it snapped somewhere and you thought there was only one way out, one way to save Aaron Krupp and his son—and to get your own name back?

"Because it would have to come sooner or later. You would have to crack under that lifelong treatment. A person can hold only so much. And it happened to snap for you while you were with Diana, trying to reason with her, having a highball to try to relax. What did she do? Did she laugh? or sneer? did she loll on the white shag rug, flaunting her beautiful

163

body, telling you how she had already made a sucker out of Norman Krupp and how she could do the same to his father—and to you too, if you didn't go away and leave her alone?"

I rubbed my eyes with my palms, trying to clear them.

"That would be enough, wouldn't it, after what you'd put up with? Enough to make you see things you'd never seen. Enough to make you pick up the whisky bottle and hit her in the head, enough to make you follow through, since you were frantic now, and grab the pillow and hold it over her face till you couldn't hold it any longer. And after that, you knew she would never steal from you again or ever bother Aaron Krupp. And you had your own name again."

The room went out of focus and I blinked my eyes to bring it clear again.

"In my book, it was no crime. I wish I was writing the book. I tried, honey. I tried to make it be Barney, with that pin that either you or Diana had bought for him and hadn't got around to giving him yet. I tried to pin it on him, and it might have worked. But I couldn't. When the time came, I couldn't do it."

I leaned back in the chair and closed my eyes, trying to relax, wishing the hospital smells would fade away and only the fragrance of gardenia stay with me. But the perfume was all gone and after a while I got up from the chair. I leaned over the bed and kissed her. She stirred slightly and sheets rustled. I straightened and Aaron Krupp's dark eyes were watching me.

"Mac," he said softly, "you know what to do. No matter how much it costs—"

"All right," I said.

I walked away and went into the corridor.

Donovan was leaning against the corner of the wall that made the nurses' alcove. Larry and the cop were gone. I walked up to Donovan.

"Where now, shamus?" he said.

I tried to grin at him, but my mouth wouldn't work.

"To find a good lawyer," I said. "Mr. Krupp is paying the bills."

Donovan was staring over my shoulder toward her room.

"Funny thing," he said. "I didn't get it put together till I went in that kitchen and found the broken highball glass—after you talked to me on the corner."

I stood there.

"Good luck, shamus," he said.

"So long, copper."

I went away down the corridor and waited a long time for the elevator.

www.ingramcontent.com/pod-product-compliance
Lightning Source LLC
Chambersburg PA
CBHW020645180626
46816CB00003B/1131